The Quiet One

He wasn't the loudest man in the room.
Just the one she couldn't ignore.

Cameron Lane
Stone House Editions
2025

The Quiet One

He wasn't the loudest man in the room. Just the one she couldn't ignore.

Published by
Stone House Editions
Stories of the Heart, the Spirit, and the Unknown

eBook ISBN: 979-8-9992336-1-5
Paperback ISBN: 979-8-9992336-8-4

For inquiries or permissions, visit:
CameronLaneBooks.com

Printed in the United States of America and other locations worldwide.

Table of Contents

PART I – Arrival & Resistance

Chapter 1 – The Chapel and the Woman...1

Chapter 2 – Blueprints & Boundaries..8

Chapter 3 – The Man in the Window...16

Chapter 4 – Opposition Files..26

Chapter 5 – The Library's Silence...37

PART II – Collision & Unraveling

Chapter 6 – A Study in Contrast...49

Chapter 7 – What's Left Unsaid..59

Chapter 8 – The Drawing Room..70

Chapter 9 – Hollow Places...79

Chapter 10 – Things We Don't Fix..87

PART III – Openings & Erosion

Chapter 11 – The Language of Stillness..96

Chapter 12 – Unmarked Blueprints...107

Chapter 13 – The Room She Never Entered..119

Chapter 14 – Outside the Frame...128

Chapter 15 – The Kiss..137

PART IV – Collapse & Clarity

Chapter 16 – The Distance Between Hands..146

Chapter 17 – The Reassignment..160

Chapter 18 – Resignation...172

Chapter 19 – Rituals of Letting Go...183

Chapter 20 – The Presentation..192

Chapter 21 – The Door He Left Open...204

Chapter 22 – The Quiet One...212

Epilogue – After Stillness...222

About the Author...231

Book Club Discussion Guide...232

For the ones who never needed to speak first—
but were always felt.
For the quiet ones,
who loved without fanfare,
and stayed without asking to be seen.

Chapter 1

The Chapel and the Woman

Julian Vero wipes a layer of salt-dusted ash from the altar rail. The grain of the wood resists him, as if reluctant to yield its years. He doesn't flinch at the creak of the warped floorboards or the cold that seeps through the seams of the chapel's stone. Here, at the edge of the sea, St. Avila's leans against the wind like a tired sentinel, forgotten by time but not abandoned by him.

He uses hand tools only—chisels, brushes, worn cloths. No music. No phone. His silence is ritual, not avoidance. Each gesture is deliberate: not efficient, but reverent. To sand the wood is to trace it. To clean the brass is to listen.

The townspeople think he's restoring the chapel for them—for history, or legacy, or tourism. He lets them think that. But this is not a restoration; it is a reckoning. He is not rebuilding. He is remembering. And he will not name what, or who, he's remembering—not even to himself.

Across town, Sera Linden arrives with a canvas tube of

blueprints, a black tote bag, and a schedule so tightly gridded it could hold a city together. She steps off the taxi into Wintermere's brittle light. The town, coastal and out-of-time, smells like seaweed, salt, and flaked paint.

She notes the cracked shutters, the slanted signage, the threadbare flags in shop windows. It's not just quaint—it's stubborn. A place that doesn't perform its decay for charm but clings to it like an old coat too well-worn to part with.

Sera doesn't dislike it. She doesn't like it either. She is trained to see potential. Her eye scans for lines, angles, load-bearing weaknesses. She thinks in timelines and grant cycles. But in her chest, something falters. Wintermere isn't just in need of transformation. It's resisting it.

She checks in at the Harbor's Edge Inn, answers a quick call from her supervisor, and steps back out into the air. There's a damp chill. She tightens her scarf and sets out in search of caffeine, unfamiliar with the fact that some changes begin not with design, but with interruption.

Crossing in Stillness

Mariner's Rest was wedged between a shuttered florist and a barbershop whose striped pole no longer turned. Its front door resisted the pull, creaked once, then let go with a chime that was more hesitation than welcome.

Sera stepped inside and was met with warmth—not just of temperature, but of history. The air carried notes of worn wood, roasted beans, and something faintly herbal—rosemary, or maybe thyme baked into yesterday's scone. The walls, painted the amber of aged honey, bore the weight of time: crooked art prints, pinned postcards, a sagging shelf of forgotten paperbacks and tide-warped field guides.

She took it in like a breath she hadn't known she was holding.

At the counter, she ordered black coffee—no cream, no flourish—and chose a seat near the window, where a shaft of late-day light cut across the tabletop. She unrolled the town map from her tote and let it settle across the grain. Her fingers hovered over the lines—not marking, just following. The streets curved with more memory than logic. The river bent like someone uncertain.

She wasn't trying to orient herself. She was listening.

Behind her, the door opened again. She didn't turn.

But something in the space shifted.

She caught the movement first in the reflection of the pastry case: a man entering, cradling a wooden crate. His steps were quiet, unhurried. Not careful—natural. He moved like someone accustomed to stillness, not seeking it.

He wore a coat that had seen salt and time. Boots scuffed from use, not affectation. Hands wrapped around the crate's worn edges like he'd built it himself. No earbuds. No phone. Just the soft rhythm of presence.

Julian.

He nodded at Gwen, the owner, who returned the gesture without words. Familiarity that needed no announcement.

As he passed behind her, Sera didn't look up. But she felt him. That strange electricity—not of touch, but of being noticed noticing. The air cooled perceptibly. Or maybe it just stilled.

She allowed her gaze to drift—not directly, not rudely—but enough to catch his shape through the glass, through the edge of her periphery. Shoulders straight, but not rigid. A face made for quiet—strong around the eyes, unhurried in expression. There was nothing soft about him, but nothing defensive either. The kind of man who didn't explain his way into a room.

Julian didn't glance her way. Didn't pause. But she saw the moment he registered her too—the infinitesimal hitch in his gait, a recalibration in the air between them.

Not recognition. Not interest. Something quieter.

As if they were both reading the same line in a book neither had opened aloud.

Then he moved on, disappearing toward the back, the crate lighter by something quietly left behind.

The door eased shut behind him. Not a slam, not even a creak. Just the soft exhale of old wood returning to rest.

Across the café, the red-haired barista paused mid-wipe. Her hand stilled. Her eyes lingered on the door a beat too long—just enough to betray that something had registered. She wasn't smiling. Not quite. But something in her expression had gentled.

Sera saw it.

Not as a woman sizing up another, but as a witness to shared recognition. A presence had passed through this place, and it had touched more than one person. Without touching anything at all.

The light felt different now. Brighter, yet dimmer. More focused, yet slightly off-center. Like a lens just nudged out of alignment.

The ceiling fan ticked above—though it didn't spin. A teaspoon was set down with careful quiet. Someone near the window cleared their throat.

Everything was ordinary.

Everything was altered.

Sera stared down at the map again. The grid blurred slightly, the lines too rigid now for the town they represented. Her thoughts, usually clean and charted, had drifted. She was suddenly aware of her breath. Of the way her fingers pressed together. Of the space across from her—a chair that hadn't been occupied, but now felt vacated.

She didn't know his name. Didn't want to. Not yet.

But she would remember the silence that passed between them.

Not a moment. A note.

Low, sustained. Unresolved.

The Lane Out

Julian steps into the narrow passage behind *Mariner's Rest*, his sleeves dusted with flour and crate splinters. The air meets him in layers: salt, damp wood, the metallic trace of rain not yet fallen. It touches the skin and then keeps going, settling into the seams of clothing, into bone.

The alley does not open. It compresses. Two buildings lean inward as if conspiring, one of brick, the other clapboard, their walls bowed from time and weather. Paint peels like old bark. A corroded pipe drips steadily onto moss-darkened stone.

Julian moves through the lane without haste. His boots make no sound, the crate carried with the silent precision of someone who has long known its dimensions. He doesn't think of where he's going. He moves through Wintermere the way water slips through a notch—by memory, not map.

A tabby cat darts between refuse bins, glances at him once, then vanishes. A door slams somewhere in the middle distance. A gull cries. The church bell strikes the hour, though he does not count it. Everything feels slightly muffled, like the town is listening inward.

He doesn't look back. He never does.

But something follows him—not footsteps, not memory. A pressure. A trace. The stillness from the café has not dispersed. It lingers behind his ribs, subtle and ambient, like a shift in weather before the storm announces itself.

She had been there.

Not studied. Not noticed in any performative way. Just registered. A presence quiet enough to bypass conscious appraisal, but not so faint as to escape his field entirely.

Not a face.

A temperature.

He adjusts the crate. The side digs into his forearm where a nail juts slightly, an imperfection he hasn't fixed—not out of neglect, but because knowing it's there helps him carry the weight evenly. Small habits. Quiet balances. He doesn't question them.

Down the alley, a rusted spiral stair winds up to a door that no longer opens. Weeds sprout from the stonework. A window above is fogged with years. These details do not need his attention. They are part of the route, embedded in his rhythm.

And yet—today—they feel different.

Not changed.

Tuned.

As if the air had caught its breath the way he had, just briefly, back in the café. As if it had watched her too.

He turns the corner without hesitation.

Doesn't pause. Doesn't define.

But something, unspoken and delicate, folds itself into the pace of his leaving.

And the lane, which for a moment had expanded—had felt less like an exit and more like a corridor of pause—narrows again behind him. Like lungs returning to their usual shape after having held breath too long.

Chapter 2

Blueprints & Boundaries

The meeting is held in the Town Hall annex—a low-slung building with faded siding and a history of water damage. Inside, the fluorescent lights hum faintly overhead, casting a sterile, too-white sheen across the beige-paneled walls. Foldable chairs are arranged in rows, their metal legs scraping audibly against linoleum as attendees shift, lean, or cross their arms. A coffeemaker gurgles in the back near a folding table stocked with Styrofoam cups, powdered creamer, and a tray of cookies no one touches.

Sera Linden stands at the front, beside a pull-down projection screen that curls slightly at the edges. Her heels clicked softly against the floor as she advanced her slides. Each one is crisp, precise—renderings of pedestrian walkways, seaside viewing decks, artisan storefronts tucked beneath refurbished colonial cornices. Her voice is practiced but not rote, confident but not forceful. She talks about integrating heritage with modernity, enhancing access without disrupting charm.

"This isn't about replacing Wintermere," she says. "It's about revealing it."

She believes that. Believes it enough to have spent months on this project—refining, modeling, anticipating friction and designing for it. But belief alone does not fill the room. She can feel it: a stiffness, not aggressive but present. Arms folded. Brows furrowed. Postures that lean away instead of forward.

A man near the back coughs into his hand, murmurs something to the person next to him. Another flips through the packet she distributed at the door, not reading, just rustling. The atmosphere is neither hostile nor open. It's something quieter. Mistrust that's earned its place over time. Not a wall, exactly. A reluctance.

Sera advances another slide. The pointer finds its mark. "The coastal overlook will preserve natural sightlines while incorporating subtle architectural cues from the town's original maritime structures."

Someone coughs again. A woman in a quilted vest scribbles in the margins of her copy. From the side of the room, Councilman Liam Decker offers a small nod of support, but doesn't interrupt.

Sera continues. The content is right. The tone is right. The strategy is right.

But the room is not with her.

Not yet.

A Name Unspoken

Sera advanced the slide with a steady hand. Behind her, the projection screen glowed a soft, institutional blue—her bullet points clean, her diagrams meticulous: "Revitalization Goals," "Historic Integration," "Coastal Access Enhancements." Her tone held steady—clear, confident, deliberate. She'd presented to city councils twice this size—with double the tension and half the patience. But here, in Wintermere's annex, she felt something else.

Not hostility. Not even skepticism. Something quieter. Older. A current beneath the floorboards.

The room didn't breathe with her. It braced.

The annex itself did no favors. Beige walls, buzzing fluorescents, metal chairs with plastic backs that flexed just enough to feel unstable. The carpet had the trampled look of something laid down in the Reagan era and never revisited. The scent was part mildew, part burnt coffee, with a trace of sea brine that seemed to cling to the seams of the windows.

As she spoke—terms like "pedestrian corridor," "historic façade preservation," "stormwater mitigation"—she saw the shifts. Not major. But definite.

An older woman in the second row adjusted her cardigan, again and again, though the room wasn't cold. A man in a fleece vest leaned back with arms crossed and a jaw set just enough to say he'd already made up his mind. Someone near the side wall tapped a pencil, not taking notes, just marking time. The projector whirred on, indifferent.

"We envision a walkable downtown that honors Wintermere's architecture while creating space for renewal," Sera continued. "Our plan includes low-scale artisan retail fronts, coastal overlooks that retain public access, and full cutoff lighting to minimize glow—"

"She doesn't know the way tide works here," a voice muttered.

It was low—intended only for the person beside him—but audible. The man wore a weathered Mariners cap turned backward, not in defiance but in habit. His tone wasn't antagonistic. It was conspiratorial. The kind of voice that didn't need to be loud to be agreed with.

A woman near the front raised a hand, but her expression made clear she didn't expect much. "Parking's already tight. Where do tourists go?"

Before Sera could answer, another voice cut in from a few rows back. "We don't need this place turned into Newport," he said. "We like the dark."

A soft ripple of laughter rose—gentle, genuine. The kind of laugh that said: *Exactly that.* Sera smiled professionally.

"Light pollution is absolutely a concern we've addressed. The proposed lighting includes warm-spectrum LEDs with directional control."

But it didn't land. Her words were precise, reasonable. But the room was drifting. Not against her—but around her. A quiet stiffening, like a tide pulling backward before the wave.

On the dais beside the councilmembers, Liam Decker leaned forward. Early thirties, collared shirt without a tie, and the only one on the panel who looked like he still believed meetings could lead to progress. He gave her a small nod—supportive, half-apologetic.

"We're not trying to erase anything," Liam said, his voice calibrated for calm. "This isn't about paving over the past. It's about helping the town evolve—keep what's essential, and make it stronger."

There was a pause.

Not long. Just long enough.

From the back row, a voice emerged—unhurried, gravel-edged. "Ask Julian," the speaker said.

Two words. That was all.

But the name landed like a dropped tool in a quiet room.

There was no gasp. No shift in posture. But something unspoken passed from person to person, a subtle recalibration of attention. Sera felt it before she fully understood it: the presentation hadn't just hit resistance—it had encountered gravity.

Someone else, older—maybe mid-seventies, sharp-eyed with a face like driftwood—added, "He won't come down unless it matters."

No elaboration. No need.

Sera didn't recognize the name. But she recognized what the room did when it was said. Conversation quieted—not silenced, just…refocused. The energy condensed.

They hadn't said *Julian Vero*. Just *Julian*. Then, *he*. And the room understood.

There was no reverence in it—not the worshipful kind. It was the kind of respect you didn't speak aloud because it didn't need to be spoken. A man whose absence carried as much weight as most people's presence.

A name not deployed for approval, but as proof.

Sera, silent, reached for her notebook. She turned to a fresh page—not for minutes or data, but for what mattered more: the undercurrent.

In the margin, she wrote one word:

Julian

Then underlined it—once, with the slow certainty of someone who knew they'd be returning to it later.

Not as reference.

But as consequence.

Marginalia

The chairs scrape backward in tired harmony, the sound of retreat without applause. A collective exhale of civic duty done—not completed, not resolved, but endured. Papers rustle. Zippers whisper. Boots scuff tile. The room begins to loosen its shape.

Sera stands still for a beat longer than necessary. Not frozen—just suspended. Watching the slow dispersal of townspeople as if their movements might offer some final clue, some code to be deciphered in the gait of a retired fisherman or the way a clerk from the hardware store folds his agenda in thirds. They do not.

Conversations begin again in hushed fragments—low murmurs, abbreviated nods, the habitual tones of people retreating to the familiar. A few avoid her gaze altogether. Others meet it with the closed politeness of the unreceptive: not hostile, just unreachable for now.

She thanks the council chair—mechanically, professionally. Collects her clicker. Unhooks her laptop from the HDMI cord. These gestures are rehearsed. Executed without hesitation. But her thoughts have wandered far from timelines and stakeholder approvals.

That name still echoes—not aloud, but within.

Julian.

It pulses like a drumbeat felt rather than heard. Not intrusive, but inescapable.

She returns to her chair—not because she needs to, but to anchor herself. To pause before facing the fog outside. The room is thinning now, voices receding down the hallway. Only the municipal heating speaks in soft clicks and groans, struggling to fend off the chill that lives in the bones of old buildings.

Her notebook lies open. Half a page remains from her final talking point—a bullet list of follow-ups, action items, people to contact. All structure. No clarity.

She picks up her pen. Not to check anything off. Not to draft next steps.

Just one word—Julian—written in the margin, above the fold. Not a header. Not a list item.

A clue.

She doesn't know who he is. Not yet. Hasn't met him. Hasn't heard his voice or seen how he holds his eyes when someone challenges him. Doesn't know if he'll resist her plans or reshape them, if he'll matter once or become a thread that pulls the whole thing loose.

But she knows how the room changed when his name surfaced.

How the conversation didn't just mention him—it bent around him.

That kind of influence doesn't come from title or tenure. It's earned slowly, or not at all. And in Wintermere, that kind of weight is not bestowed lightly.

She closes the notebook.

Outside the annex, fog smudges the town's edges. The streetlamps flicker against the damp. For a moment, she watches the harbor dissolve into the gray.

And somewhere between the map and the margins, she knows the story has shifted.

Unreceived

Sera walks alone back toward the inn, coat collar turned up against the damp. The streetlights flicker. Porch lights reveal more absence than invitation.

The meeting hadn't gone badly. But it hadn't gone right either. She knows that kind of silence—the polite kind that masks withdrawal. She's heard it in boardrooms, foundations, city councils. It's the kind that doesn't say no aloud—because it already has, privately.

Back in her room, she unpacks but doesn't settle. The word is still there in her mind. Not the proposal. Not the data.

Just one name.

Julian.

It was the only thing the room had accepted without defense.

Chapter 3

The Man in the Window

The fog had thinned by late afternoon, but the air still held a quiet weight, like a room that hadn't been spoken in all day. Sera walked without direction, her boots pressing into the soft grit where sidewalk gave way to shoreline. She'd told herself it was just a break—fifteen minutes away from survey flags and stakeholder spreadsheets—but her pace said otherwise. *Not rushed. Not wandering.* Just distant enough to suggest she was walking something off.

Wintermere had begun to fold in on itself for the day. A clatter of shutters in the harbor. A **CLOSED** sign flipped at the bakery with a flick of the wrist. The tide rocked the boats with a sound too slow to be called rhythm. Smoke from an unseen chimney drew a loose thread in the air and then dissolved. These were not the signals of nightfall. Just the slower breath of a town that had learned how to quiet itself before the dark arrived.

She veered toward the bluff—habit, not plan—and followed the dirt path that curved above the bay. The wind met her there. Not sharp, but constant. She pulled her coat closer.

That's when she saw it.

Movement, barely perceptible, through the warped glass window of the chapel. She slowed. Stopped. The building stood like it always did—angled against the coast, its paint dulled to a color between white and seafoam, the wood trim warped from salt—but now it wasn't still. Inside, behind the pane, someone moved.

She stepped to the side, half-shielded by the slope and a low hedge of winter-thinned shrubs. It felt wrong to watch. But she didn't stop.

Through the streaked pane, a figure knelt before a panel of stained glass. Gloved hands moved with quiet certainty, adjusting—no, tending—to the colored fragments. Julian. She didn't know it yet, not with proof. But she knew.

He didn't glance up. Didn't sense her. His focus was complete, not rigid but rooted, the way someone kneels not to fix something, but to listen to it. As if the window had a memory he was there to honor, not overwrite.

His posture struck her first. Precise, yes. But not performative. There was a stillness to it that wasn't fragile. Something reverent. Not the chapel's, she realized. His.

The light from the west caught the edge of the glass he was working on, spilling amber and cobalt across his sleeve. For a moment, she could see nothing else—just the color moving across his arm as he worked.

She watched for less than a minute. But in that minute, something in her recalibrated.

Not her thoughts. Not her plan.

Her attention.

She turned before he could notice—though she sensed he wouldn't have looked up even if she'd stayed. The wind picked up again as she stepped back toward the main road, the chapel dipping out of view.

But the shape of that stillness stayed with her.

And somewhere between the tide and the rooftops, she knew the name she'd written in the margin was not a footnote. It was a hinge.

A Casual Inquiry

Back at *Mariner's Rest*, the late afternoon has surrendered to a soft dimness. The café windows reflect more of the inside than the outside now—hints of lantern light catching in the glass, the harbor beyond dissolving into slate-gray dusk. Sera stands at the counter, arms resting lightly on its worn wood surface, trying to appear casual, maybe even bored, as Gwen moves between tables with the slow, practiced rhythm of someone who's wiped down this same space every day for the last twenty years.

Gwen, a woman in her late fifties with short gray-streaked hair and a sturdy cardigan that might as well be part of her uniform, doesn't look up when Sera speaks.

"So… who's working on the chapel?"

She says it like an afterthought. Like someone asking about weather or paint color.

Gwen keeps wiping a laminated menu with a damp cloth, circular motions smooth and unhurried. "Julian," she replies, as if that explains everything.

Sera waits. But Gwen doesn't elaborate.

"He fixed the bell tower last winter," she adds, finally. "No one asked him to. Just brought scaffolding and got to it."

Sera raises an eyebrow, surprised by the directness, but also by the tone—not admiration, exactly. Something quieter. Resigned? Familiar?

"Was it... his job?"

This time, Gwen straightens up, glancing toward the back of the café as if checking for something, or perhaps someone who might overhear. Then she shrugs. A gesture so even and uncomplicated it feels like the delivery of a local proverb.

"Not officially," she says. "But some folks don't wait for permission."

The words land more sharply than Sera expects. There's no edge in Gwen's voice, but there's something embedded in the line. A boundary. A truth Wintermere seems to accept without question. Sera files it away without knowing why. She hears the sentence again in her head, but differently now:

Some folks don't wait for permission.

She doesn't quite know what to do with it yet. It could signal independence. Or rebellion. Or a brand of stubbornness more potent than either.

She nods thanks, moves back to her corner table with her tea cooling beside her laptop. But her focus has shifted. She doesn't open her spreadsheets. She doesn't refresh her inbox. She just watches the harbor lights blink on, one by one, and thinks about a man she hasn't met, a chapel window half-seen through glass, and a town that bends around his name.

Julian.

She says it silently, testing the syllables like a stone in the palm. Not an answer.

A beginning.

The bell above the door of *Tide and Texts* gives a muted chime as Sera steps inside, brushing a thin film of coastal mist from the shoulders of her coat. The bookstore is narrow, warmly lit, and quietly cluttered. Shelves lean just slightly with age, crammed with everything from local history pamphlets to used mysteries and atlases with frayed corners. The air smells of yellowed paper, sea salt, and faint pipe tobacco—though no one smokes here anymore.

Behind the worn oak counter stands Harris, the owner—late sixties, thin-framed, half-untucked shirt beneath a well-worn cardigan the color of wet bark. His reading glasses perch at the tip of his nose, though he's not currently reading. Instead, he's unpacking a small box of returned books with the kind of reverence most people reserve for heirlooms. He doesn't look up when Sera enters. He doesn't have to.

"Looking for overlays or ordinances?" he asks, already reaching for a set of rolled documents behind the counter.

"Zoning maps," Sera says. "And any historical site records for the bluff. There was some mention of maritime chapels in one of the old planning files."

Harris pauses.

Then, without commentary, he pulls out a folio from the box on the floor. "Found this in the return bin this morning," he says, brushing a speck of dust from the spine. "Doesn't belong to any of our regular stacks. Thought it looked like your kind of thing."

He holds it out without explanation.

Sera takes it carefully—an oversized folio, its cover a faded charcoal gray with no title, just the impression of where a label might've once been. The edges are soft with age, the binding threadbare. She opens to the first page. 19th-century architectural studies—mostly maritime chapels scattered along the Eastern seaboard. Floor plans, sketches, elevation cross-sections. She flips slowly, her eyes scanning not the printed material, but the handwritten notes in the margins.

Graphite. Deliberate. Unhurried.

The annotations are… unusual. They don't just describe; they interpret. *"Unbuttressed apse—either deliberate minimalism or post-storm modification."* On another page: *"Roof pitch fails to account for coastal wind shear—likely aesthetic over function."* And then—*"Rose window design inconsistent with coastal wind logic."*

Sera freezes. It's not the content that stops her. It's the tone. Or rather, the absence of tone. The precision. The clean, slanted script that doesn't announce itself, doesn't overstate, but somehow feels like it carries weight beyond the words.

She's seen this handwriting before. Not exactly—but close enough to matter. It mirrors a note she came across in the council file on the chapel. A small correction about timber rot thresholds, made in the margins of a report no one else had touched in years.

There's no name here. No signature or monogram.

But she knows.

It's Julian.

She doesn't know how she knows, and still, she does. Not a hunch—an alignment. The notations in this folio don't read like academic commentary. They read like stewardship. As if the writer wasn't analyzing history, but quietly tending to it.

She looks up at Harris. He's already returned to sorting books, saying nothing more.

"Can I take this?"

He nods. "It was unclaimed. I'd rather it be in hands that want to understand."

Sera thanks him, tucks the folio under her arm, and steps back out into the evening fog. The folio is heavier than it looks. Or maybe it's just that something in her understanding of this town has shifted again. Not because of what's written—but because of who didn't sign it.

And somehow, that absence says more than any name could.

The Shape of Anonymous Presence

The wind rises just after midnight—thin and rhythmic, tugging at the corners of the inn like a lullaby sung through a screen door. Sera sits cross-legged on the end of the narrow bed, the folio spread open before her, lit by the amber-glow lamp on the side table. The room is hushed but not silent—pipes ticking faintly in the walls, the occasional groan of old floorboards settling as if the building, too, were exhaling.

She's read through the folio twice already, but her eyes return to the margins. It's not the content that holds her now—it's the manner of it. The way the notes appear. Not in every spread. Not in any predictable place. Sometimes a full sentence, sometimes just a phrase. Often tucked near the binding where the eye wouldn't naturally fall. They read like thoughts half-meant to be found. Half-meant to be kept hidden.

None of them boast. None draw attention. They never say *I think* or *I suggest*. There is no first person. No agenda. Just statements—observations rendered with such calm clarity they land as fact, even when speculative.

She finds herself whispering one aloud. "*Lateral bracing*

absent—likely lost to storm, or never there at all."

It's not just the insight. It's the restraint. The refusal to overreach. These are not the markings of a man eager to impress. These are the annotations of someone compelled to understand, even if no one else ever would.

She flips back to the note about the rose window. She can almost see him now, standing before the real one—gloved hands held behind his back, studying the angles not for beauty, but for contradiction. For the place where intention met failure, or failure revealed something truer than intention.

What unsettles her isn't his intelligence. It's his anonymity.

People who know things—who fix things—tend to announce themselves. To take credit, even quietly. A comment in a meeting. A name on a report. A photograph. But Julian does none of that. He builds. He repairs. He annotates. But he does not claim. There is no signature. No calling card.

Just presence.

The kind that enters without knocking and leaves the air changed.

It's not mystery for mystery's sake. She can feel that clearly. Julian isn't trying to be elusive. He's simply unwilling to be misread. There's a difference—and it's a rare one. He's not hiding. He's withholding. Choosing silence where others would insert explanation.

She closes the folio gently, running her thumb once along the frayed fabric of its spine.

Who restores without credit? Who gives without appearing? Who speaks only in the small spaces left by others?

She asks herself, without even realizing the question has

formed: What does a person like that want?

And why, she wonders, does that question feel more intimate than any she's asked aloud?

Curiosity with Edges

It's late, and the desk in her inn room is cluttered with the artifacts of a structured mind unraveling—maps, survey overlays, printouts of heritage guidelines, her project notebook splayed open like a wound. A cup of tea, long gone cold, sits forgotten beside her elbow. Outside, the fog clings low across Wintermere, wrapping streetlamps in gauze. The only sound is the hush of distant waves, more sensed than heard.

She turns a page in her notebook, intending to list site considerations for coastal setbacks, but her pen stills. The space in the margin calls to her—not the lined space of bullet points, but the edge. The in-between.

Her hand moves before her mind quite does.

Julian—chapel? folio? bell tower?

She stares at the name. Not in search of meaning. In search of why she wrote it that way—like a line item in an unknown equation. She's not compiling facts. She's triangulating.

It's not romantic. Not really. There's no blush in it. No thrill. It's not even personal. It's architectural. Structural. As if by mapping his presence, she might better understand the hidden beams of the town itself. Because clearly, he is one of them— something silent holding the place upright.

And yet, the more she tries to chart it, the less linear it becomes. Every new piece of information about Julian—his hand in the folio, the bell tower he repaired without being asked, the window he restored with no fanfare—only deepens the ambiguity.

There is no file on him. No plaque. No position. But there is impact. Weight. The kind that rewrites rooms without ever speaking.

She thinks of the town meeting—how the room had shifted around his name like a landscape around a boulder. He hadn't been present. But his absence had a density all its own. Reverence wasn't quite the word. Nor fear. It was something else. Something earned.

What unsettles her most is not the lack of facts. It's the *feeling* of familiarity. As if she's encountered him before—not in this town, but in some other shape. A type. A pattern.

Someone who moves beneath, behind, and still leaves everything changed.

She doesn't yet close the notebook, and doesn't cap the pen. For a long moment, she watches the name in the margin. Not bolded. Not circled. Not emphasized.

Just... there.

A quiet tether between knowing and not.

And it stays with her the rest of the night—not the name itself, but the shape it makes in her thoughts.

Like the outline of something foundational, half-buried in the design.

Chapter 4

Opposition Files

The town hall is full—standing room only. Folding chairs line the scuffed linoleum like mismatched teeth, every one occupied. The buzz of old fluorescents overhead blends with the low murmur of preemptive frustration. It's not loud, but it's layered—snippets of argument, sighs of fatigue, the occasional hiss of velcro on a windbreaker peeled back in tension. Wintermere has shown up not just for discussion, but for reckoning.

The agenda is printed in neat black type on white paper, stacked at the entrance beside a dish of peppermints no one takes. Phase II of the revitalization project. It sounds neutral. Bureaucratic. But no one in the room believes it's neutral. And nothing in Wintermere is ever just procedural.

Sera stands near the front, hands folded over the edge of the podium, her notes a fortress of clarity she's no longer sure will hold. She scans the crowd—not for allies, not even for opposition, but for temperature. The kind that can't be read in facial expressions, only in the way people sit: how forward their shoulders lean, how still their fingers rest, how little they blink.

This is not a room ready to be convinced.

She can feel it in the acoustics—the way sound lingers a second too long, as if even the walls are holding their breath. A man in the back adjusts his cap. A woman near the door uncaps a pen but doesn't write. Someone shifts, chair legs screeching faintly, and the sound is sharper than it should be. These are not just participants. They are stewards. Witnesses. Owners of memory, in a place where memory often trumps momentum.

She glances down at her notes again, but the words seem thinner now. Budgetary phases. Traffic projections. Restoration incentives. Measured. Practical. Entirely beside the point.

Because what's really on trial tonight isn't funding or footpaths. It's belonging.

And belonging, in Wintermere, isn't about paperwork.

It's about who gets to define what stays.

Who decides what the town becomes—and what it refuses to be.

Sera inhales slowly. She's not nervous. Not exactly. But there's a quiet split opening inside her—a sense that she might be speaking *from* the proposal, but no longer *for* the town.

And across the crowded room, she knows—before a single word is said—that this meeting won't be about metrics.

It will be about memory.

And memory, she's learning, doesn't yield easily.

Fault Lines in the Open

The meeting begins in orderly fashion—gavel tap, roll call, approval of minutes. But it doesn't stay orderly for long.

Sera steps to the front with practiced calm, slides her updated proposal onto the overhead screen, and begins the presentation. Her voice is steady. Her pacing deliberate. The new phase emphasizes historical fidelity, traffic flow improvements, and sustainable design. She highlights local labor. Notes the grant window closing. Pauses at key words like *respectful adaptation* and *community stewardship.*

But the room doesn't warm. It hardens.

Questions interrupt before the second slide. Not hostile— yet—but pointed. Then come the rebuttals.

Maureen speaks first. Late sixties, wire-rimmed glasses, a scarf that's appeared at every meeting since Sera arrived. She doesn't raise her voice. She doesn't have to.

"Synthetic siding?" she asks, as if the term itself offends the paint on the walls. "We're not Disneyland. We don't need facades pretending to be us."

A murmur of assent ripples through the back row.

Then comes Dennis, the café owner from down by the docks—mid-40s, sleeves rolled, a ledger always folded in his coat pocket like a lifeline.

"Foot traffic keeps the lights on," he says flatly. "Sentiment doesn't pay rent. We need a trail that gets visitors to the harbor, not another season of preservation theater."

The room teeters—caught between nostalgia and necessity, between shingles and solvency. Between what once was and what might survive.

Sera interjects—not defensively, but carefully. She presents a compromise: synthetic siding only on the rear-facing wall, textured to match original clapboard. Reinforcement of original façades with modern support structures behind. Visual integrity maintained, safety enhanced. A balance of old and new.

But as the words leave her mouth, they feel… brittle.

Like glass under tension.

Like sense without resonance.

And she realizes, mid-sentence, that she doesn't know anymore whether she's *advocating* for the town—or simply *representing* the firm that sent her.

The difference scrapes.

Her voice remains calm, but internally, a fracture widens. She scans the crowd and sees not opposition exactly—but detachment. Not coldness, but a kind of conditional patience. As if they're waiting for her to stop performing fluency in a language they never asked her to speak.

They don't see her as a threat. But not as one of them, either.

Not yet.

And in that quiet estrangement, a thought creeps in before she can dislodge it:

They're not listening to what I'm saying. They're listening for who I sound like.

And right now, she doesn't sound like the town. She sounds like a liaison.

A proxy. A voice in a borrowed room.

And that truth lands harder than any formal opposition. It doesn't shout. It doesn't accuse.

It just stands quietly in the back of the room.

And waits.

The Door That Opens

It happens mid-discussion—just after a contractor begins citing cost differentials between poured concrete and reclaimed brick. The words are still in the air when the double doors at the back of the hall creak open.

The sound is quiet. But it travels.

Heads turn. Conversations still.

Julian steps inside.

No announcement. No hesitation. Just presence.

He wears what he always wears—an old field coat, sea-stained and soft at the seams, the collar brushed with the faint white bloom of dried salt. His boots carry the dull clatter of someone who didn't dress for the meeting, but showed up anyway. Not defiant. Not careless. Just… untouched by performance.

He does not sit. He does not need to.

People shift—subtly, instinctively—making space along the wall as if rehearsed. No one gestures. No one speaks. They just move. It's not deference exactly. Not status.

It's gravity.

And that, more than anything, is what Sera feels first.

She doesn't notice his face. Not right away. What she notices is the room—how it folds around his entrance like fabric drawn toward a heat source. A quiet blooming of attention. The kind that doesn't rush. That waits.

The kind given to someone whose silence has history.

Julian leans lightly against the back wall, arms crossed—not in defensiveness, but rest. He watches, not intently, but fully. There is no note-taking. No subtle nodding. Just stillness with weight.

Councilman Liam glances toward him. The moment hangs there, unforced.

"Mr. Vero," he says, the tone a blend of acknowledgment and invitation. "Do you have a view on this?"

Julian's voice is low, calm. Not loud, yet it carries—like water under stone.

"Some things don't need to be rebuilt," he says.

"They need to be remembered."

A pause. No dramatics. Just the cadence of belief.

"The stone remembers."

That's all.

But it's not *all*.

The words hang in the air—not as argument, but as shift. They don't follow anyone's point. They don't contradict or concede. They simply land.

Unhurried. Undeniable.

Sera hears it first as a tone—resonance before meaning. And then she feels it: the echo of his voice threading through everything she's just said, everything the room has pushed and pulled against.

Not a counterpoint.

A reckoning.

And as the silence deepens, she realizes: this is not the voice of someone trying to sway.

This is the voice of someone who speaks only when speaking is the last, most necessary thing left to do.

And the room listens.

Not out of respect.

Out of recognition.

Weight Without Volume

The words settle before they echo.

No one speaks. Not right away.

A breath holds in the collective chest of the room—not stunned silence, but something slower, deeper. As if the walls themselves need a moment to absorb what's just been said.

It's not lofty. Not poetic for its own sake. There's no flourish in the phrasing. No drama in the delivery. It's just… final. As if it had already been true and Julian simply named it aloud.

Sera doesn't react at first. Not outwardly.

But something inside her does.

Because she knows that voice—not in familiarity, but in frequency. The tone of it vibrates in a place she hadn't realized was tuned to listen. It's the same quiet resonance she felt in the chapel window. In the marginal notes of the folio. In the ghost-print of his name written beside her own.

And now, hearing it fully—undiluted, deliberate—she recognizes the connection her mind had only hinted at before. He's not an idea anymore. He's here. Whole. Spoken.

And yet, he hasn't explained a thing.

That's what strikes her most.

Julian didn't debate. Didn't posture. Didn't ask.

He *offered*—a statement of principle wrapped in the language of memory. No agenda. No technical detail. Not even a suggestion.

Just the invocation of weight.

The tension in the room doesn't disappear—it *reorganizes*. Hard edges soften. Postures relax. The business owner who'd argued fiercely moments ago now shifts his stance, not in concession, but in reconsideration. Maureen, the preservationist, lowers her notes.

Even the fluorescents seem quieter.

No one calls for a vote. No one tries to rebut.

Councilman Liam closes his binder halfway, fingers resting on its spine like someone pausing a conversation that's grown too large for the room.

What Julian has done isn't persuasion.

It's disruption without violence.

Immovability without resistance.

Presence without volume.

And it works.

Not because people agree. But because they remember.

And somehow, in that remembering, the urgency to decide—to declare, to draw lines—dissolves just enough to make room for something else.

Sera watches him from where she stands, words she never got to speak still folded inside her notebook. And in the absence of noise, in the hush his presence has made, she feels it:

The shift isn't about siding or budgets or trail routes.

It's about *who holds the past*—and how that shapes what can come next.

And in that moment, she isn't sure if Julian just challenged her proposal… or quietly gave it a spine.

What Lingers After

No vote is taken.

Councilman Liam, still holding his binder half-shut as if uncertain whether to reopen or close it for good, simply clears his throat and says they'll revisit the proposal at a later date—"with adjustments." No timeline. No motion. Just that word: *later.*

It's enough.

The formal end of the meeting is announced, but the room

doesn't respond with the usual shuffling and scrape of chairs. There is no rush to the exits. Just a slow, reluctant rising—like a congregation dismissed not with triumph or failure, but something more private. Reflection. Recalibration.

Conversations that had once buzzed now taper into murmurs. A few linger by the walls. Others gather their coats in silence. Even the most vocal critics from earlier seem to move with a kind of subdued thoughtfulness, as if unsure how to carry forward after what just *was*.

The air still holds the shape of Julian's words, like a bell's tone long after it's rung.

The stone remembers.

Sera doesn't move. Not right away.

She remains near the front, her notebook still open in her hands. The page she'd planned to read from—her structured remarks, carefully plotted to balance feasibility with sentiment— sits untouched. A few sentences are underlined. A bullet point half-crossed. But the center of the page is blank.

Because she hadn't spoken.

Because *he* had.

And that, somehow, had been enough.

She tells herself it doesn't matter. That her input can come later. That the project isn't derailed, just… paused.

But something deeper hums beneath that logic. A feeling she can't quite name.

She finally closes her notebook, slow and deliberate. The sound is soft, but final.

Julian is already gone.

She hadn't seen him leave. No dramatic exit. No glance

toward her. Just absence, folding back into the air the way he had entered—without signal or ceremony.

But the *effect* remains.

Not just in the room.

In *her*.

She feels changed by proximity. Not dazzled. Not infatuated. But interrupted—in the way only a rare kind of presence can interrupt you: not to take something from you, but to show you something you hadn't realized was missing.

Not truth. Not clarity.

Attention.

His words hadn't demanded anything. They had simply named something the room already knew but hadn't voiced. And now, she wonders: Is that what it means to speak with weight? Not to persuade—but to *place* something into the room so precisely, so calmly, that everything else must rearrange around it?

She gathers her coat but doesn't leave.

Not yet.

Because she is still circling a realization that refuses to land cleanly:

That this man—this quiet figure the town instinctively makes room for—does not assert authority.

He *becomes* it.

Not through volume. But through timing.

Through silence held until it matters most.

And now, a thought rises in her—not bold, not urgent, but persistent:

I want to matter to him.

She doesn't know what that means.

Not yet.

But she knows it isn't professional. And it isn't romantic.

Not exactly.

It's something rarer.

She wants to matter in the way that makes a person like Julian *speak*. In the way the chapel made him kneel. In the way memory made him enter a room and alter its course with a sentence.

Not to impress him.

To *register*.

And for now, she has no map for that.

Only the echo of his voice.

And the way the room had changed because of it.

Chapter 5

The Library's Silence

The morning arrives gray-edged but bright, the kind of coastal light that doesn't warm so much as it clarifies. Sera walks through it with a steady pace and a deliberate gait that almost—but not quite—disguises a certain internal recalibration. She tells herself this is a return to routine. A morning task, nothing more. Data, maps, the topography files she'd flagged two days ago. Something measurable. Something professional.

The streets of Wintermere are quiet, the post-storm hush of a town caught between seasons. A gull calls overhead but goes unanswered. A trash bin lid clatters in the wind, then stills. She passes the bakery with its windows fogged from the inside and turns left toward the library, eyes on the ground, coat collar high. She doesn't look up at the bluff. Doesn't glance toward the chapel. Not because she's forgotten.

Because she hasn't.

The Wintermere Library sits just above the slope of the harbor road, a building that looks like it was placed rather than built—cut stone, tall windows, two brass doorknobs that shine faintly even in muted weather. There's no sign announcing it. Just a low-arched plaque embedded in the wall beside the door: *Wintermere Library, Est. 1889.* Beneath it, someone has taped a handwritten note: *Quiet Requested. Patience Required.*

She enters with a push that requires more force than expected. The heavy door resists in a way that feels intentional, like it has always preferred those who insist gently.

Inside, the air is different—drier, warmer. The scent of aged paper, floor polish, and the faint ghost of beeswax wrap around her as she steps inside. The hush is not imposed, but grown—like a living thing cultivated in the corners. A library of presence rather than absence.

She straightens her posture slightly as she approaches the front desk. The librarian, a woman of indeterminate age with a sleek gray braid and wire glasses worn low on her nose, is rearranging a stack of old microfilm sleeves. Her glance is brief but precise.

"I'm looking for the coastal topography maps," Sera says, voice low but clear. "Bluff line overlays, water encroachment— anything from the last ten years."

The librarian's hand pauses mid-stack. Then, with a small flick of her wrist, she gestures toward the reading room.

"Already being reviewed," she says.

Sera follows her glance.

Then stops.

Across the main floor, past a row of sunlit periodicals and beside a long oak reading table, sits Julian.

He's turned slightly away, absorbed, the full curve of the map unfurled before him like a tide partially withdrawn. His reading glasses rest halfway down his nose, catching a glint of morning light that spills through the eastern window and pools across the table in a slow, golden ellipse. One hand rests lightly on the page's curled edge. The other traces a ridge line with the flat of a fingertip—careful, not possessive.

He hasn't seen her.

Not yet.

Sera hesitates—not out of indecision, but because something in her still wants this to be about work. About overlays and bluff lines and the firm logic of municipal thresholds. She could wait. She could return later. She could pretend she didn't see him, take a different archive and chart her day around anything else.

But she doesn't.

Because the part of her that wants answers—the one that studies more than maps—is louder now. Not brash. But insistent. Like wind under a door.

She exhales quietly. Then steps forward.

And for the first time since arriving in Wintermere, she does not ask herself whether this is the right moment.

She simply walks toward it.

Meeting Without Formality

Julian does not look up right away.

He's aware of movement—the soft rhythm of footsteps padded by caution, not uncertainty. A pause near the end of the table. The air shifts almost imperceptibly, not as if someone entered the space, but as if the space remembered how to make room.

His hand stills on the edge of the map.

Then he lifts his gaze.

They meet each other's eyes—directly, openly—for the first time.

There's no startle in it. No delay. Just a calm recognition that lands with the quiet authority of something overdue but not misplaced.

Sera doesn't smile. Doesn't speak immediately. But something in her posture softens, just slightly—like a tent pulled one stake looser. The moment holds, and then, with a voice measured enough to leave nothing assumed, she says:

"May I?"

Julian regards her without tilt or squint. His eyes are steady—not cold, not inviting, just clear. He doesn't nod right away. He looks at the map, then at the seat across from him.

He gestures toward it—not with flourish, but with the kind of precision that suggests intention behind every movement.

"Watch the upper corner," he says. "It curls."

His voice is low. Grounded. Unforced.

He slides the map toward her as she steps around the table. Their fingers move at the same time—hers to adjust the edge, his to keep it flat. They don't touch. But the space between their hands becomes suddenly charged—like a proximity sensed, not seen.

Sera takes the seat.

It creaks slightly beneath her, an old library chair not built for elegance but for patience. She adjusts the page just enough to keep the alignment true. Julian shifts his weight a little, settling again into the posture of someone who'd never planned to be interrupted—but isn't unsettled by it either.

She places her notebook to the side, unopened. No need for

performance. No compulsion to announce her purpose. There's nothing formal here—no exchange of names, no justification of presence. Just a shared attention, given freely.

Julian speaks again, not looking up from the map:

"That bluff line's out of date. The runoff carved deeper after last spring's thaw."

Sera nods, instinctively. "I noticed that on the southwest trail. Sediment drifts into the low slope near the storm drain."

His eyes lift to meet hers again.

Briefly.

And it's different this time.

Not recognition. Not surprise.

Agreement.

Like two notes sounding the same frequency—separate, but momentarily in resonance.

No one says more. There's no need.

Around them, the library hums in its own quiet rituals—pages turning, floorboards shifting in slow protest, a pencil somewhere scratching out the marginalia of another quiet life.

They sit at opposite sides of the same map.

But the space between them does not feel like distance.

It feels like the exact measure of what it is:

An unspoken invitation. Unrushed. Unnamed.

Understood.

The Texture of Voice

Julian listens before hearing.

Not to her words—they come later—but to the way her presence folds into the quiet. Some people enter a room like punctuation. Sera doesn't. She moves like syntax—deliberate, necessary, without noise meant for effect.

When she speaks again, it's to clarify a contour line just north of the bluff's elbow—one that dips unnaturally, suggesting erosion or a poorly charted culvert. Her finger traces the slope. Her voice follows.

"It's likely tidal seep. But I'd want to see the spring levels before calling it permanent."

That's all she says.

But Julian hears it.

There is no overreach in her tone. No anxious proof-of-competence, no affected lightness. She speaks with that rarest of registers: clarity without self-regard. The words land as observations, not as claims. Her voice doesn't seek to impress. It simply belongs.

He studies the space she leaves between her sentences. It is not caution. It is accuracy.

She speaks, he realizes, the way some people build: not to display strength, but to test where the weight will hold.

And quietly, without meaning to, the phrase forms in his mind.

The sound of shoreline—unclaimed.

He doesn't know why the thought arrives. It's not poetic. Not metaphorical. Just true. That's what her voice feels like. Like water over sand before the land decides what shape to keep. Something in motion, but not in search.

Across the table, Sera doesn't notice him studying her. Or if she does, she doesn't let on.

She's focused again, eyes scanning the northern ridge line

now, where the tree coverage breaks. She leans in just enough to suggest that she has forgotten to be careful.

And Julian watches—not her exactly, but the way the air changes in response to her presence. There is no tilt in the room, no charged hush. Just balance. That's what strikes him. She doesn't ask the quiet to make space for her. She arrives already fluent in it.

He shifts his gaze back to the map, not to hide anything, but because holding eye contact feels like speaking—something neither of them seems willing to do just yet.

And still, they are speaking.

Every time she offers an observation, he answers with silence—but not withholding. It is a shared silence. The kind that listens back. The kind that says: *I heard you. I agree.*

For Sera, the realization comes more slowly.

At first, she's simply relieved by the lack of small talk. No name exchange. No anchoring of identity in job titles or affiliations. But as the minutes pass, she begins to register something deeper.

It isn't just that Julian doesn't fill the air. It's that she doesn't feel compelled to either.

And that, she thinks, is its own kind of intimacy.

She speaks again, lower this time, adjusting the map's northern border. "I think the ridge shifts here," she says, tapping the paper. "But the lines don't account for wind shear. Could be a cartographic overlay from a non-coastal firm."

Julian glances over. Then gives a small nod.

"You see it," he says.

Not praise. Not surprise.

Just acknowledgment.

And for the first time in weeks, Sera feels a kind of steadiness she can't trace to any decision or plan. No argument was made. No opinion won. But something essential has been accepted.

Not her work.

Her way of seeing.

Working in Parallel

They settle into the kind of silence that doesn't announce itself.

No truce has been declared. No roles defined. But gradually, without any overt shift, they begin to work in tandem. The map unfurled between them becomes less a boundary and more a bridge—something shared, not divided. Their gestures never clash. When one reaches for a reference page, the other waits. When one adjusts an edge, the other anticipates the weight.

It isn't seamless. But it is fluent.

Sera flips the overlay to a translucent sheet showing water encroachment patterns from 2006. Julian aligns the corner with two fingers and sets a brass paperweight in place—a faded compass rose behind worn glass. Their hands pass close, not brushing, but aware. Always aware. The choreography is unconscious, but meticulous.

She speaks only when necessary—naming dates, flagging notations. He responds in short phrases or quiet nods. Once, they both reach for the same coastal data card, and their fingers graze the edge of it at the same time. Neither pulls back. Julian simply releases his hold. Sera doesn't thank him. Doesn't need to.

The stillness between them is not sterile. It hums.

Around them, the library continues its private murmurs. A page turned in the alcove. A chair shifting near the biography shelves. Somewhere in the back, a drawer clicks closed with the soft finality of routine. The world is not watching them. But it holds them, quietly, as if aware that something too fragile for naming is being formed.

Sera glances up once—not at him, but at the light across his shoulder. It moves differently now, slanting eastward, casting a warm stripe across the table where the compass paperweight sits like an artifact. The map's translucent overlay shimmers faintly beneath it. For a moment, she forgets the scope of the project. The reports. The tension. She is only aware of how their two shadows fall across the same border line.

Julian, in turn, does not look at her. But he registers the change in her breathing—the quiet slowing that signals presence. Not performance. Not calculation. Just presence.

He does not know what she wants from the map. But he knows she's not here to take from it.

And that matters.

He's worked near others before—builders, engineers, town clerks hunched over ledgers. But always there had been something to deflect. To compensate for. A noise. A need. An urgency to prove. But this woman does not ask to be granted space.

She simply fills it, carefully.

He finds, to his quiet surprise, that he doesn't want her to leave.

Not because of who she is. But because of what she doesn't disrupt.

And Sera, eyes still on the map, feels the same pull—but names it differently. To her, it is the realization that this moment is unrepeatable. Not because it is momentous, but because it is balanced.

Two minds, briefly aligned.

Two presences, equally restrained.

She turns a page, then pauses—not to say anything, but to stay where she is a moment longer. The silence between them, like a shared bench facing the sea, continues.

Not empty.

Shared.

The Moment That Holds

Eventually, the edges begin to lift.

The paper, worn from use and touched by the warmth of morning light, begins to curl again at the upper corner—just as Julian said it would. Sera reaches for the paperweight, gently repositions it, then pauses with her hand resting against the curve of the map's rolled edge.

They've said very little.

But it no longer feels like they haven't spoken.

Julian leans back slightly, folding his reading glasses and setting them near the edge of the table with quiet precision. He doesn't check the time. Doesn't stand. Just shifts, as if listening inwardly to the closing of a door he didn't open.

Across from him, Sera begins to roll the map. She does it carefully, not as a gesture of departure, but of closure. Not an end, but a recognition that the moment has reached its natural pause. The silence doesn't resist the action. It deepens it.

She finishes, ties the ribbon of archival linen around the roll, and sets it between them. Her fingers rest there for a second longer than needed.

Then: "Thank you," she says.

Not for the map. Not for the guidance. For the space. For the stillness shared without permission or instruction.

Julian nods—once, without smile or deflection.

"You saw what mattered," he says.

The words are simple. But they land.

Sera feels them settle beneath her ribs—not because they praise, but because they reflect. Because they name something without claiming it. And because he says them not to compliment, but to acknowledge.

She doesn't answer. Just holds his gaze for a single beat longer than courtesy would require. Then gathers her notebook and rises.

He doesn't follow her with his eyes as she walks away. But she doesn't mistake that for indifference.

Some people look to hold on.

Julian looks to release what doesn't need to be kept.

At the door, she pauses—not from doubt, but awareness. She doesn't turn back. Just breathes once, steady and full.

And steps into the morning.

The library door closes softly behind her.

Inside, Julian remains seated. One hand still on the table, fingers relaxed, palm open.

He does not reach for the next document. Does not resume his work.

He just sits for a while longer.

Not to reflect. But to register.

Later, neither will recall precisely what was said—only fragments. A phrase. A gesture. A single shared correction on a bluff line. But both will remember the feel of it. The rare balance of two minds meeting in the same quiet, at the same depth.

Not a beginning.

Not quite.

But something subtle, structural. A seam stitched into the architecture of a morning neither of them planned.

It will return to them differently in memory—his as a stillness not broken, hers as a silence that did not ask for shape.

But for now, it remains unspoken.

Unfinished.

Intact.

Chapter 6

A Study in Contrast

The morning arrives dim and undecided. Mist curls low across the chapel grounds, not dense enough to obscure, but enough to blur the edges of things—tree limbs, fence posts, the faint silhouette of the sea beyond. It is the kind of weather that doesn't declare itself, only lingers, as if waiting to see what the day decides to become.

Sera walks the path with steady steps, her boots soft against the wet grass, clipboard tucked under one arm, tablet case cinched tight against the salt-damp air. She is dressed for professionalism, in muted colors and practical layers, each chosen to signal capability without inviting conversation. Her breath leaves faint clouds in the air as she exhales—more from focus than cold.

She tells herself this is just a site survey. One more piece of the process.

A scheduled walk-through. Nothing more.

But she knows better. The map she carries is not the one that matters today.

Ahead, the chapel rises out of the fog like a memory half-returned. Its roofline cuts a quiet silhouette against the pale sky, the siding washed to a bleached gray that once resembled white. The windows do not shine. They absorb light. Its angles are not severe—but steadfast. The structure does not resist time. It stands beside it.

Julian is already there.

He crouches low near the stone foundation, a brush in one hand, the other resting lightly against the wall as if listening through it. Dust clings to his sleeves. His coat bears the same marks as always—wear, salt, repetition. He does not look up when she approaches. Does not announce himself.

He has been working since before the light fully arrived.

There is no greeting.

Just the quiet rhythm of motion and breath and the soft scratch of bristle on stone.

Sera slows, not out of hesitation, but from a need to match the frequency already present.

For a long moment, neither speaks. The air moves around them—fog curling past boot soles, wind brushing against the bare limbs of a nearby tree. A gull passes overhead and does not cry out.

The chapel watches. The ground holds still.

Then, without looking at her, Julian stands.

Brush in hand, dust on his palms, he wipes the edge of the lintel above the chapel's side entrance. His touch is not reverent. It is familiar.

Sera opens her clipboard. Taps the tablet once to wake it. The glow is faint against the morning gray.

"We'll begin with the perimeter," she says, eyes on the screen. "Document slope, drainage, access points."

Julian doesn't respond right away.

Then, quietly, still facing the stone, he speaks:

"My grandfather laid this lintel. After his wife died."

Sera blinks, then glances up.

But Julian is already turning away, beginning to walk the edge of the structure with the same calm gait as always. As if he hadn't said something that rearranged the ground beneath her feet.

She doesn't answer. Doesn't press.

She simply follows.

And the silence that stretches between them isn't empty.

It's waiting.

Stone and Blueprint

They walk the chapel's outer edge in parallel, tracing the building's foundation as if circling something long buried rather than merely assessing it.

Sera names the features aloud as she notes them, her voice steady, clipped by focus:

"Grade slope: uneven—retaining wall needed."

"Entry threshold too narrow for ADA compliance."

"Signage—heritage-style, low-profile, preferably wood or weathered metal."

She taps a few entries into her tablet.

"Lighting to be minimal—low-glow bollards or inset LEDs."

She is speaking for the project. For the plan. For the layers of oversight that will eventually review every word, every figure, every inch of pathway. Her cadence is professional, firm, but not forceful. A rhythm she knows well.

Julian walks beside her without comment. His hands remain in his coat pockets, dust still clinging to the creases in the fabric. He listens—not to respond, but to absorb. His attention is not on the words. It is on the chapel itself.

They reach the side wall—the one sheltered most from the coastal wind—and Julian slows. He brushes his hand along the weathered stone, fingertips finding a groove in the mortar no blueprint would register.

He doesn't speak again. He doesn't need to.

Sera remembers what he said a few minutes earlier—before they began their loop around the chapel. About the lintel. About his grandfather. About the woman who had died.

It's not a story. It's a placement.

A piece of history set like a stone into the building itself.

She looks up at the lintel differently now—not as an object to preserve or a detail to document, but as a marker of unspoken grief. A gesture not meant for visitors or future grants or architectural review boards.

Something human.

Uncataloged.

Sera feels the weight of her clipboard shift slightly in her hand, though she hasn't moved.

"Do you want it preserved?" she asks, not looking at him.

Julian's answer comes after a pause, quiet and even.

"It'll hold," he says. "That's enough."

She doesn't press.

Some elements in a project resist categorization.

Some aren't meant to be protected by policy.

They endure by choosing to.

And not all of them are made of stone.

Language of Purpose

They continue around the chapel's perimeter, the ground soft beneath their steps. The fog has begun to lift in places, thinning into ribbons that drift between gravestones and tree roots, revealing the landscape in slow increments—like memory returning not all at once, but in fragments.

Sera moves with intention. She gestures toward the bluff, then the path that curves between the trees. Her words are composed, measured. But there is a quiet urgency beneath them.

"We're looking at low-impact trails—stone dust or permeable pavers. ADA-compliant slopes. Wayfinding markers that tie in with the historical palette. There's a grant window closing in six weeks, so we need to finalize bids before then."

Julian doesn't interrupt.

He walks beside her, eyes on the land, not the screen in her hand. He studies the slope beneath the old oak near the chapel's northeast corner, watches the way the wind pulls the grass in long, slow lines. He kneels briefly to test the soil near the foundation, then stands again without comment.

Sera continues.

"We're proposing directional lighting—nothing intrusive. Warm-spectrum LEDs, full cutoff fixtures to minimize upward glow. Just enough to keep the trails usable after dusk. The site could support small gatherings—local musicians, seasonal programs. Maybe even a restoration workshop series. There's cultural funding for that."

She doesn't expect him to object.

She expects him not to answer.

But he does.

Not immediately.

And not to her.

He stops walking.

They're near the bluff's rise now, the chapel behind them, the sea just visible through the thinning mist.

Julian turns slightly, his hand grazing the edge of the stone wall that marks the chapel's boundary.

"Some places," he says, voice low but clear, "aren't meant to be lit."

It isn't said harshly. There is no resistance in his tone, no challenge. Just a kind of quiet finality—a belief that has not asked for approval.

Sera stops too. Her breath clouds once in the air before fading.

She doesn't answer right away. Not because she disagrees— but because she's trying to decide if she does.

She looks around. The chapel grounds in this light are subdued, but not bleak. The silence feels intact. Intact in a way that artificial light might fracture. It's not just the darkness Julian protects. It's the integrity of what exists *before enhancement.*

Still, she says, gently, "People need access."

Julian's gaze doesn't move from the bluff.

"And some things need protecting from being made

accessible," he replies.

They aren't arguing. Not exactly.

But something has shifted.

This is not a conversation of facts. It's a conversation of values.

Her language is purpose. His is protection.

Between them, the chapel stands—its mortar aging, its lintel holding, its silence unbroken.

Coastline Questions

The path veers toward the bluff, narrowing as it rises. Grass gives way to packed earth, flattened in places by foot traffic, worn smooth where wind and rain have done their work. The ocean begins to speak below them—not loudly, but in long vowels, low and patient. A sound between breath and memory.

They walk without speaking for several steps. The silence is no longer shared in comfort. It pulses now, stretched between differing truths. Not tense, but taut.

At the overlook, they pause.

The chapel sits behind them, half-shrouded in fog and morning light, but here the sea is clear. The view is long and open—water stretching out to a pale horizon where color and sky meet in a kind of uncommitted blur.

Sera steps forward, near the edge where the wooden railing leans slightly from time and weather. She scans the line of the coast, eyes narrowing. Already, she's envisioning the possibilities: a tiered deck, curved benches made of reclaimed wood, discrete lighting tucked along the rail, interpretive signage etched in bronze. A place to linger. To take photos. To be.

She gestures toward the water, tablet still in hand but forgotten for the moment.

"What do you see?" she asks.

Her voice is not performative. She's not probing for poetry. It's a real question, shaped by genuine curiosity. Perhaps even the beginning of concession.

Julian steps up beside her, but he doesn't answer immediately.

The wind moves past them, brushing their coats, lifting Julian's hair slightly at the edges. He places one hand on the railing—not to steady himself, but as if grounding a thought.

His eyes track the horizon.

Then, after a long moment:

"A place that gives no answer."

Sera doesn't turn to look at him. But something in her stills.

It is not the response she expected. Not metaphor. Not resistance. Just a truth—not hers, but real.

For Julian, the sea is not open. It is unknowable. Not a vista, but a memory that has no interest in being decoded. Something ancient. Something that doesn't explain itself to observers or planners.

To Sera, it has always been the opposite. An invitation. A canvas. A way forward.

Opportunity, not opacity.

She doesn't refute his words. She simply breathes them in.

There is something about standing here, beside someone who sees the same thing differently, that makes her feel less certain—but more aware. Like a building being assessed from a new angle, its symmetry called into question.

Neither of them speaks again for a while.

But the silence now is less about stillness, and more about recognition.

Not of agreement.

Of difference.

Unspoken Recognition

They begin to walk back, not in sync, but near enough. The distance between them is neither widened nor closed—it simply adjusts, like a thread slackening without breaking.

The fog has mostly lifted now, revealing more of the chapel and the slope that cradles it. The light is soft, slanting in from the east, catching on the stone lintel, the weathered clapboard, the rusted hinges of the side door. The chapel looks older in this light. Or truer.

Sera slows near the front steps. She doesn't climb them. Just studies the doorway.

Julian remains behind her, half-turned toward the bluff they just left. But his eyes find her profile—steady, thoughtful, a tension held just behind the line of her mouth. She's still in the stance of a professional—clipboard tucked against her side, shoulders square—but there's something else now. A pause that doesn't belong to protocol.

She's seeing it differently.

The place.

Maybe even herself.

Julian doesn't speak. He watches.

And in her silence, he hears something unfamiliar: not agreement, but consideration. She is not conceding. But she's listening.

That is enough.

Sera senses him behind her but doesn't turn. Instead, she looks once more toward the chapel wall—the lintel above the side door. She doesn't touch it. But she registers it. Not just the material. The story. The placement. The kind of history that doesn't ask to be preserved, but insists on being remembered.

Then she glances over her shoulder—not directly at Julian, but in the direction he'll take when he walks away.

He meets her gaze—not sharply, not with intensity. Just a look held a beat longer than necessary.

It is not flirtation. It is not challenge.

It is recognition.

They do not agree. But they see each other.

She offers a small nod. The kind that doesn't signify closure, only that something has been marked.

Julian returns it. Just once.

They part without resolution, without summary. No lines drawn. No conclusions reached. But something has shifted—quietly, undeniably.

Not in the land.

In the space between them.

The kind of shift that doesn't announce itself, but waits.

Waits to be remembered.

Chapter 7

What's Left Unsaid

Night in Wintermere folds in quietly, without ceremony. The wind brushes the edges of the inn like a visitor who won't knock—just lingers at the threshold, asking nothing but leaving presence behind. Outside, the trees lean and creak with the kind of language no one speaks anymore. Not quite warning. Not quite song.

Inside, the rooms are dim. Sera hasn't turned on more than a single lamp, the kind with a soft amber shade that casts light sideways, not out. The floorboards hold a gentle chill that rises through her socks. The air smells faintly of cedar and sea salt, and something warmer—perhaps from the old books on the windowsill, perhaps from warmth left by the earlier sun.

She sits on the armrest of the couch, one knee pulled in loosely, phone in hand. Not scrolling. Not checking. Just holding it, as if its weight might clarify something.

The room is quiet. But not the kind of quiet that brings peace.

It's the kind that presses at the corners. That listens back.

Her thumb hovers over the screen. The voice memo app is open, blinking like a small, expectant eye. She's recorded these before—messages for Em, her older sister. They talk less now than they once did, but still enough to sustain the tether. Em lives two time zones away, with children and a life that runs on schedules Sera has never memorized.

She's not sure what she wants to say. Not really.

She could talk about the chapel. About the walk along the bluff. About the man who said less than anyone else and somehow rearranged the air around him. But it feels too loaded, too revealing, even if she frames it as casual.

Still, she presses record.

Her voice is quieter than usual. Not because she's hiding— but because she's thinking even as she speaks.

"He doesn't flirt. Doesn't hover. Just… exists.

Like stone. Or tide. Constant. Quiet."

She stops the recording. Rewinds. Listens.

The first time, it sounds like an observation. The kind of thing you say about someone you've noticed, not someone who's noticed you.

The second time, it sounds different.

Not just about him.

About her.

About something shifting, quietly, without permission.

She doesn't send it.

She sets the phone facedown on the worn wooden table beside her. The screen disappears, but the feeling doesn't.

She isn't falling.

She knows the shape of that. She's lived it—twice, maybe

three times, depending how you count. Falling has an arc, a rhythm, a thrill edged with danger. Falling is loud.

This is something else.

Something slower. Something more structural.

Not a collapse. An unseaming.

She leans back, lets her eyes fall closed. The wind hums against the windowpanes like breath against skin. The night holds.

And in that quiet, she realizes:

She's not falling. She's unraveling.

The Deleted Message

She imagines Em's voice before she ever hears it.

Not because she plans to send the message—she won't—but because the conversation has already started in her head. That's how it goes with Em. Even with miles and years between them, her sister's voice still shows up in moments of ambiguity, like a lamp switched on without asking.

"Sounds dangerous. You always fall for the loud ones."

Sera can almost hear the inflection: breezy, amused, a spoon stirring tea in the background. The kind of comment meant to nudge, not judge. Em never said much outright, but she knew how to underline a truth without lifting the pen.

The loud ones. Yes. That was her pattern.

Men with big ideas and quick mouths. Their confidence arrived first, their insecurities trailed behind like loose threads they hoped no one would pull. She had fallen for declarations. For easy intensity. For men who made her feel temporarily visible by speaking as if she were already known.

Julian is not that.

Julian doesn't declare.

He doesn't hover, doesn't fill silence with performance.

He simply occupies space—with presence, not persuasion.

And that is more disorienting than charm ever was.

She picks up the phone again. Her voice message still sits there, unsent, a blinking icon like a door she hasn't quite opened or closed. She taps play.

"He doesn't flirt. Doesn't hover. Just… exists. Like stone. Or tide. Constant. Quiet."

She listens as if someone else recorded it.

There's a pause before "exists."

A softness on "quiet" she didn't hear the first time.

It isn't the words that betray her. It's the tone.

Not romantic. Not breathless. But something far more dangerous—exposed. As if she's speaking from a place just beneath her usual defenses, where thoughts aren't yet curated into narrative.

She imagines Em listening. Tilting her head slightly, smile curling, picking up on things Sera didn't intend to admit.

"You always fall for the loud ones."

That voice again. Not judgmental. Just accurate.

But this time, it's not a warning. It's a recognition.

And what unsettles Sera most is that she doesn't know who she is in this new pattern. If Julian is the quiet one, what does that make her?

What version of herself does she become in his presence— less armored, more watchful, unsure whether she's being seen or simply revealed?

That's what she doesn't want to explain. Not to Em. Not to

anyone.

Not yet.

Because once it's named—this shift, this gravity, this internal rearranging—it becomes real. And real things demand shape. Direction. Consequence.

She stares at the screen.

Then deletes the message.

Not from indecision. Not from pride.

But because it says more than she's ready to know.

And suddenly, the room feels smaller. As if the walls have drawn a fraction closer.

She sets the phone down face-first on the side table and exhales without realizing she'd been holding anything in. The wind brushes the eaves again, like a breath on glass.

Outside, nothing has changed.

Inside, something has loosened.

The Absence That Echoes

The message is gone. But the silence it leaves behind does not settle.

It lingers.

Not as regret—Sera is past that—but as a kind of residue. A trace. As if deleting her voice has somehow made it louder in the room.

She stands. Not suddenly, not with purpose—just the kind of rise that comes when stillness starts to press from within. The lamp on the table hums faintly, a low filament sound that would be swallowed in any busier place. But here, in Wintermere, in a room that smells of wood and wool and restraint, every sound has presence. Even the absence of them.

She crosses to the small alcove where a tray of glasses and a carafe sit beneath the window. Fills one. Doesn't drink it. The movements are familiar, almost ritual, but without faith. Just gestures to fill space.

In her reflection on the window, she catches a glimpse of herself—not clearly, but enough. There's a look she recognizes and resists: inward-facing, unslept, softer at the edges than she used to be. It unsettles her, not because she's changed, but because she hadn't noticed it happening.

She leans on the windowsill with one hand, her palm flat.

The wind rustles again. The same wind that moved through the chapel grounds that morning. The same that passed over Julian's shoulder while he stood by the bluff, speaking of places that shouldn't be lit.

She doesn't remember his exact posture. But she remembers the stillness of it.

That's what stays with her.

His hands, steady on stone.

The pause before he speaks.

The deliberate economy of someone who doesn't fill silence because he respects its shape.

She's spent years learning how to lead conversations, how to ease tension with context, how to interpret hesitation as something needing to be fixed. But Julian's silences don't need repair.

They anchor him.

And somehow, they are beginning to dislodge her.

Not violently. Not in dramatic shifts.

But slowly. Subtly. Like a shoreline reshaped by tide.

She steps away from the window and carries the untouched water to the table. Sets it down without meaning to. She doesn't sit. She just lingers, caught between thoughts.

There's nothing to name. Nothing to act on. No flirtation. No suggestion. No boundary crossed.

And yet the weight of it is real.

Presence, she thinks, can be its own intimacy.

A kind that asks nothing—but alters everything.

She turns off the lamp.

The room goes dim, then darker still as her eyes adjust. She doesn't rush to bed. Doesn't reach for a book or distraction.

Instead, she stands there.

Not looking out. Not looking in.

Just listening to the quiet he left behind.

Unraveling in Quiet Places

The lamp by the bed casts a soft amber pool over the coverlet, but Sera doesn't turn the light off. She sits with her legs drawn up, one knee loosely crossed, a folded sheaf of papers resting against her thigh. Julian's map sketches—he had lent them to her without ceremony, as if trusting her with them required no explanation.

One sheet is thinner than the rest. A rough elevation of St. Avila's chapel from decades ago, pencil lines clean and measured, the inked notations in someone else's hand—maybe his grandfather's. The proportions are exacting. The slope of the roof, the narrow arched windows, the thick lintel over the entry door. No embellishment. Just care.

She studies the drawing the way one might study the face of someone they no longer remember clearly—searching for intention behind shape.

Her finger moves just above the surface, tracing without contact. The silence is different here, different from the silence Julian carries. His is composed, deliberate. This one is atmospheric, heavier. The kind of silence that collects in your joints after long choices.

She lets herself lean back, papers still in her lap, eyes open. What unnerves her isn't that he's done something—but that he hasn't. No gestures. No implications. No edge of flirtation. He's simply been—consistently, attentively, without expectation.

And somehow that's more disarming than any approach might've been.

There's a structure inside her—a framework built over years from necessity and control. Plans, deadlines, language sharp with purpose. The scaffolding of someone who had learned how to be admired without being truly known.

And now, that structure is loosening.

Not collapsing. Not yet. But shifting.

She reaches for her journal, the one she keeps zipped inside her work bag. Opens it. Stares at the blank page.

Then closes it again.

Not because she has nothing to say—but because what she feels resists transcription.

Words would only reduce it.

She lies back. Lets the sketches fall gently to the floor beside the bed. The wind outside stirs the old trees, brushes against the glass like a thought trying to form.

She closes her eyes.

This isn't falling.

It's softening.

And that, somehow, is the more dangerous thing.

Distance and Intimacy

The next day, around midday, Sera steps out of the bakery with a bag of coffee beans and two folded maps tucked under her arm. She isn't thinking of him—at least, not actively.

But then: there he is.

Across the narrow street, stepping out of the general store with a canvas bag looped over one shoulder. There's flour dust on the hem of his sleeve, a carton of nails visible in the bag's mouth. He's walking in no particular hurry, as if the day moves through him, not the other way around.

He sees her.

And nods.

No words. No expression beyond the nod. No echo of the map or the chapel or the silence they'd shared. No acknowledgment of shared presence.

And yet—somehow—everything is acknowledged in that restraint.

He doesn't pause. Doesn't double back. Just keeps walking. A quiet rhythm, uninterrupted.

Sera stays still.

Something in her stirs—not anticipation, not longing. Just... recognition. Like passing a place you've dreamed about and realizing it's real. A feeling not of proximity to someone else, but proximity to something inside yourself you didn't know had gone quiet.

She doesn't call after him. Doesn't linger.

Just walks on.

But she feels it—that internal shift. Small, but irreversible.

Not a turn toward him. A turn toward herself.

And for the first time, she wonders:

Does he delete things too?

Words he almost says.

Moments he doesn't name.

Messages never sent—not because they were too much, but because they were already understood.

She passes the florist's window. The glass fogged from inside. A rack of postcards sways slightly in the breeze that threads the main street. Everything looks ordinary. Uninterrupted. But inside her, the air feels different. Rearranged.

There's no soundtrack. No smile pressed against memory. Just that one small gesture—his nod—and the precise weight of it.

She walks a little farther, then stops without meaning to. Standing in the shadow of a shuttered shop, one hand brushing the edge of a bench not meant for sitting long. She doesn't sit. But she doesn't move either.

The moment isn't over yet. It's echoing.

And when it finally settles, she exhales quietly. A breath she hadn't noticed holding.

No revelations. No conclusions.

Just a still point in the center of her day.

And the faint, unspeakable awareness that something has aligned.

Not between them. Within her.

She resumes walking.

This time with no maps in her hands.

Only questions she's not in a hurry to answer.

Chapter 8

The Drawing Room

Sera hadn't meant to be out this long. She'd walked to clear her head—around the bend by the post office, past the shuttered bookstore, up toward the bluff road where the ocean mist clung low like memory—but movement had turned into drift. Something about the rhythm of footfalls and the bite of salt air had steadied her. Or maybe she'd just wanted to avoid stillness.

The sky had already begun to dim, not with evening, but with something heavier—more pressing. She noticed the first drops too late. Not soft, not gentle. Sudden. Inevitable. A wind rose sharp from the coastline, and the clouds tore open with a sound like breath breaking.

The storm did not wait.

It hammered down with no warning, smearing the sky into a sheet of gray and noise. Trees bent at the waist. Gutters spilled over. The town reacted like a single organism—shutters drawn, sidewalks cleared, windows darkened. A fundraiser at the municipal hall was canceled. A-frame signs were snatched inside storefronts. Lights flickered across Wintermere.

She ran. Not dramatically. Just fast enough to suggest she was prepared, though her soaked hair and uneven breath told another story. Her coat—thin, wool, and ill-suited to weather like this—clung to her like regret. Her hands burned cold.

There was only one place open.

The chapel's small east door was unlocked, the way it often was during storms—intended, perhaps, for candle-lighting or prayer, though neither had been practiced here much lately. Still, the place held a kind of permission in its stone.

She entered like a secret. Quiet. Water clinging to her.

Inside: the faint scent of timber, limestone dust, and something herbal—clove, maybe. The door clicked softly behind her. Rain drummed against the windows like a thousand forgotten urgencies. Firelight flickered ahead. Not the overheads. A real fire.

Julian was there.

Kneeling by the hearth, sleeves rolled, hands smudged faintly with ash. A worn, cast-iron kettle near the flame. He looked up when she entered—not startled. Not expectant. Just aware.

He said nothing.

Just stood slowly, nodded toward the bench near the fire, then the kettle. His eyes held hers for a second longer than usual. Not with intimacy. With recognition.

She walked forward, the cold slowly loosening from her shoulders. Her soaked hair trailing rivulets down her back. The room felt both warm and unlit, a paradox she didn't try to explain.

Julian poured a second mug. Set it on the table beside her. Sat back down across the hearth without commentary.

The chapel held its breath.

And in that space between thunder and quiet, flame and

stone, they simply sat.

Not opposite. Not together.

Just near.

Refuge by Firelight

The fire crackled with the steady, uneven rhythm of old timber burning slow. Its light pushed shadows upward along the chapel's stone walls, exaggerating angles, softening lines. Outside, the rain hammered like memory—unrelenting, not asking permission. The storm was no longer passing. It was settling in.

Sera sat with both hands wrapped around the mug Julian had offered. It was heavier than she expected, ceramic with a faint hairline crack near the handle. The tea was dark and spiced— something root-based, unfamiliar but grounding. She didn't ask what it was. She didn't need to.

Julian hadn't returned to his work. He sat back on the low wooden bench beside the hearth, legs long, boots wet, arms resting on his knees in a posture that looked earned. A quiet built between them—thick, but not awkward. Just... attentive. Present.

Neither spoke. Not because there was nothing to say, but because something more essential was already happening. A permissioning. A moment offering stillness instead of exchange.

Their coats steamed lightly in the warmth. Sera's hair clung to the collar of her jacket, drying in strands. Julian, ever economical in movement, passed her a folded wool blanket that had been draped over a chair. She took it without thanks, not from rudeness, but from understanding that thanks might rupture the ease.

There were no words exchanged. No inquiries made. The usual scaffolding of small talk and social clarity fell away like damp leaves. This wasn't flirtation. It wasn't avoidance, either.

It was proximity.

Two people, side by side. Not facing each other, not deliberately turned away. Just sharing heat, and firelight, and the kind of quiet that doesn't need interpreting.

Sera exhaled slowly, unsure when she had started holding her breath. The tea warmed her throat. The blanket pulled the chill from her spine. Her body began to register safety before her mind could frame it.

Julian didn't look at her directly. But he remained open in posture, unguarded, as if presence itself was enough to account for. Not invitation. Not withdrawal.

Outside, the storm cracked—lightning splitting somewhere over the bay. Inside, the flame shifted in the hearth, casting orange against the old chapel stones.

And still, they said nothing.

Because here, tonight, being was more honest than speaking. And trust, like fire, sometimes begins in silence.

The Shape of What's Shared

The sound of rain softened, but didn't fade. It grew more rhythmic, more patterned—less assault, more presence. Like something returning, not something passing. It gave the chapel a kind of heartbeat. A perimeter of sound that made the inside feel smaller, closer.

Their first words came not as a shift, but as a drift.

Julian, still watching the fire, said quietly, "Water leaves stains in sandstone. Over time. Not because it's strong. Just... persistent."

Sera didn't turn toward him. "I've seen it in topography

shifts. Whole ridgelines rewritten over decades. Not from force. From patience."

A pause.

He added, "That's what makes it hard to repair. You don't patch sandstone. You learn to live with what the water left."

Another silence. This one longer, but not strained.

Sera glanced at the far wall of the chapel, where dark patches marked decades of weather seepage. "Some damage," she said, "becomes part of the structure."

He looked over then—not fully, but enough to register her profile, the way her eyes followed the grain of the stone. "Not all of it is damage," he said. "Some of it is memory."

They didn't speak again for a while. The tea cooled in her hands. The fire settled lower.

Then, unprompted, Julian lifted one hand and looked at it as if remembering something tactile. "My grandfather's hands were bigger. Could carry a whole beam across his back. He used to say a wall should never be rushed. That it'll tell you what it needs—if you let it."

Sera ran her thumb absently along the rim of her mug. "My mother left when I was seven."

It wasn't a non sequitur. Somehow, it followed. She didn't explain. But she added, after a breath, "She still shows up in my dreams. Always late. Always saying she meant to come sooner."

Julian didn't respond. Not with words. But his gaze dropped to the fire again, and something about his stillness shifted— slowed. It was as if he had received the story and was holding it quietly, not weighing it, not solving it. Just... keeping it warm.

The conversation didn't move forward from there. It simply

paused. As if the words had found a ledge to rest on.

They listened to the storm continue outside. The chapel stones held the heat, and the shadows on the walls moved like distant recollections.

The space between them didn't close. But it calibrated—to something mutual, weight-bearing, and unspoken.

Some moments don't grow louder.

They deepen.

Restoration and Forgetting

The fire dipped lower, its orange edges collapsing into ember. Julian stood briefly, added a single log with the familiarity of someone who had done so often, and returned to his place without fanfare. The heat lifted again, quietly, like a breath re-inflating.

Outside, the storm continued—not with violence now, but endurance. Steady rain, less wind. The kind that stayed all night and reminded you of the roof above your head.

Neither of them had moved much. Yet the space between them felt different—less like a distance, more like a field.

Julian leaned back, his voice almost lost in the hush: "Restoration isn't rebuilding. It's remembering."

Sera didn't reply right away. Her fingers had gone still on her mug. Her body leaned slightly toward the hearth, though her eyes were elsewhere—unfixed.

When she spoke, it was quieter than before. Not whispered, just reduced.

"I'm tired of forgetting."

There was no response from him. And none needed. The words hovered in the air like condensation—brief, warm, real.

For a long time, they just sat. No new subjects introduced. No need to redirect.

This wasn't conversation. It was suspension. A holding space. The kind of hour that leaves no quotable lines, but alters something imperceptible in the internal architecture of both people.

Julian didn't ask what she meant. He didn't pry, didn't tilt his head in sympathy. He simply remained—his quiet steadying hers.

At one point, they both looked up at the same time, toward the arched beam above the hearth. It bore a faint mark, an old nail hole or a weather stain, shaped vaguely like a crescent. Neither commented. But something passed between them in that gaze— not interpretation, but notice. Mutual awareness of the same unnoticed thing.

Their eyes met. Not romantically. Not weighted with expectation. Just aligned.

As if something unspoken in each had echoed the same internal note.

No chords struck.

No revelations named.

But the space inside the moment widened—and held.

The Drawing Room

Later, Sera will not remember the time exactly. Only that the fire had burned low and the storm had shifted into a soft, steady percussion on the windows—less a pounding now, more like a question repeating itself.

She hadn't moved for a while. Neither had he.

Their last words— *"Restoration isn't rebuilding. It's remembering."*

"I'm tired of forgetting."—had settled like sediment in water. Not gone, just quieted. Present beneath everything else.

She hadn't said them for a response. And none came. But what remained in the air was not absence. It was something more charged. A shared stillness that had been chosen, not fallen into.

Julian stood first, not abruptly, just a slight lean forward and the soft sound of boots adjusting. He moved toward the hearth, prodded the embers with a curved iron poker. Sparks rose, caught the stone in flicker, then faded again. He didn't speak.

And Sera was grateful for that.

Because something had changed in her—not toward him, but inward. A loosening. A shift in how she was holding herself. She realized, sitting there in the chapel's ancient hush, that this was the first space in a long time where she hadn't needed to explain her way into safety.

He had let her speak of forgetting. And had not tried to remind her of anything.

She sipped the last of her tea, now lukewarm. The ceramic felt rough beneath her fingers, like it had been made by someone who didn't care about polish, only weight.

Julian returned to his seat, no closer, no farther. A rhythm re-established. Their bodies still slightly angled toward the fire, not each other.

No eye contact. No questions.

And yet—

The air between them had been altered. Not charged with attraction, not softened by romance. But calibrated. Two solitudes occupying the same room without tension. Something very few people can do together.

When Sera finally stood to leave, Julian didn't rise.

He simply looked up. Not expectant. Not withholding.

Present.

She nodded, the kind of nod that holds nothing performative. Just: *I was here. You were here. We didn't waste it.*

And as she stepped to the door, the rain had quieted enough for her to hear the hinges creak. She opened it into darkness.

One glance back.

He was still seated. Still calm. A figure in stone and firelight.

The chapel behind her breathed as if it too had been listening.

And later, when she thought of the night, she would not recount what they said. She would not write it down.

But she would remember how it felt:

Not intimacy. Something rarer.

Interiority, shared.

Without demand. Without claim.

Just warmth.

And the decision—by neither of them—to let the moment be whole without needing more.

She would walk back through the empty streets of Wintermere, coat damp, hair drying in waves the wind had shaped. Behind her, the chapel glowed faintly—a held breath of stone and ember. Neither of them would speak of that night, not in words. But something unclaimed had passed between them, and neither reached to catch it. The storm had lifted. The silence remained. And elsewhere, in a quiet room lit by morning that did not ask for answers, Julian rose with no plan. Only a feeling, subtle and new, that something had shifted. Not in her. In him.

Chapter 9

Hollow Places

The storm had passed without apology. It had not cleared so much as receded—like grief that quiets only because it has exhausted itself. What remained was stillness, the kind that didn't comfort so much as hold its breath.

Wintermere lay rinsed. Its slate roofs glistened. Earth darkened to sponge beneath shuttered porches. The air carried a salt-weighted stillness that made even footsteps feel like intrusions. Skies above wore a flat pale indifference, the kind that leaves no impression—only light without warmth.

Julian rose early, though he hadn't slept much. Not for restlessness, exactly. Just something else. Something unnamed. He left the home without tools. No satchel of sketches, no gloves, no list tucked into his coat. He walked empty-handed through the soft-limbed streets, as though following a summons he couldn't articulate.

At the chapel steps, he paused—not out of hesitation, but reverence. There was a subtle shift in how the building met him today. It didn't invite. It received.

He reached for the door slowly, as one might approach a room where someone is sleeping, or grieving, or praying. The hinges creaked the way they always had, but today the sound seemed fuller. Not louder. Just thicker—as though the silence inside had learned how to hold it differently.

Julian stepped inside.

He didn't speak. Not yet. He simply stood there for a moment, breath anchoring, eyes adjusting. The chapel smelled of ash and rain-soaked wood, faintly threaded with the last trace of Sera's wool coat. Not perfume—memory.

The fire from the night before had long since died. But the room still held warmth. Not in temperature. In presence.

He let the door close behind him.

And then—only then—he moved toward the altar wall, slower than usual, his steps unmeasured. Not the careful gait of a craftsman ready to inspect his work. But the walk of someone unsure what the work even was anymore.

The Unspoken Question

The chapel did not look different. And yet, it felt altered in some essential register—subtler than sight, deeper than scent. Not changed. Just less expectant.

Julian moved through the nave without sound, boots brushing the stone in soft, deliberate friction. He did not scan the ceiling beams or assess the moisture in the south wall like he usually did. There was nothing technical in his gaze. No checklist unfolding beneath his eyes. Only presence.

He stopped where the wall bowed inward slightly—a fault line he'd studied a dozen times but never quite resolved. For months now, he had sanded, braced, reinforced. Measured tolerance. Monitored strain. Yet even now, with his palm pressed lightly to its surface, he sensed that something here would never settle in a structural way. It wasn't a flaw in the stone. It was a memory folded inward. A bruise that had chosen to remain.

He closed his eyes.

The wall was cool, but not cold. It met his touch without resistance. And in that quiet exchange, something in Julian softened—not in emotion, but in assumption.

He drew a slow breath and released it through the stillness. Then, without thinking whether it was foolish or strange, he spoke—not loudly, not declaratively, but as if placing a sentence into the room like a fragile object on a table.

"I still don't know what I was meant to repair."

The words didn't echo. They just hung there, suspended, as though the chapel had stopped breathing for a moment to listen.

He didn't expect a response. But he waited all the same—not for answer, but for alignment. For some internal shift that might let him name the pull that had brought him here day after day, long after the grant ended and the blueprints grew soft around the edges.

Nothing came.

And yet, the silence did not feel hollow. It felt paused.

Like a question not yet refused.

Like something waiting to be understood without being solved.

The Window

The light had shifted.

Julian turned toward the eastern window, where the afternoon sun, now muted by sea-hung clouds, slanted through the glass in softened angles. Dust hovered like silt in water. The shadows were slow-moving, not fixed—like something was still deciding whether to stay.

He reached into his coat pocket, removed a small candle, and placed it on the sill. A quiet habit. A kind of tending. The wax had been melted and reused so many times it bore no shape, only persistence. He struck a match from the inner fold of his sleeve, shielded the flame with his palm, and lit the wick. The flame stuttered, then steadied. Flickered again. It didn't brighten the room. It registered—a declaration not of light, but of presence.

That's when he saw it.

At first, it looked like nothing more than a flaw in the frame—some weather-softened warp, or a glint of old shellac. But then, as the candle's flame leaned slightly in the draft, the glass caught a shift in color.

Green.

Not the dull green of aged wood, nor the sharp hue of paint.

Sea glass.

Tucked into the edge of the window frame, barely visible unless one stood at this angle in this light, was a smooth-edged shard of pale green glass. The kind the tide rolls until it forgets it was once a bottle. The kind Sera had held loosely in her hand just two days ago, as they walked the chapel grounds. She hadn't spoken of it. Had only turned it between her fingers, sunlight spilling through the translucence. He'd noticed, then. Chose not to ask.

And now—here it was.

Pressed carefully between wood and stone, not forced but nested. A gesture left without note or claim. Not hidden, but not announced either. Just placed.

Julian didn't move closer. He didn't touch it. He only watched it catch the low light, watched the flame reflect in its curved edge like a second, smaller signal.

A part of him wanted to ask why she'd left it. Another part already knew that asking would dissolve the point. Some things weren't meant to be explained. They were meant to be received.

Sea glass.

Tide-worn. Softened by being broken. And then returned.

The Sketch

It's not there at first.

Julian doesn't see it when he enters. His eyes are drawn to the sea glass first—its placement almost imperceptible, just a glint in the window's frame. But later, as he crosses toward the back wall to check the mortar—more out of habit than need—he notices something resting on the hymnal shelf.

A sheet of paper. Unframed. Charcoal on coarse fiber stock, not smudged by handling. Left deliberately.

He doesn't touch it. Not yet.

It's a figure, viewed from behind. A woman—shoulders slightly turned, hair gathered loosely at the nape, as if caught mid-movement or pause. The lines are soft but sure, edges smudged as though they were meant to dissolve into the light. There's no signature. No initials. But he knows immediately.

It's her.

Sera.

Drawn in a way that holds back every gesture of vanity. There's no staging. No dramatized silhouette. Only stillness and turn. As if the sketch isn't about the woman herself—but about the moment just before she disappears around a corner, or turns to face the wind.

He steps back—not because he's startled, but because the intimacy of the thing expands suddenly in the room. The quiet gets thicker. Denser. As though the chapel walls have recognized something in their midst and are holding their breath.

Julian studies the drawing again.

He hadn't seen it the night before—not during the storm, not when they shared tea in the firelight. Which means...

She must have come back.

This morning. Early.

Before anyone else.

The thought brushes against him like mist—fine and barely there, but impossible to ignore. She had returned, not to meet him. Not to be seen. But to leave this. Quietly. Without explanation.

Not for praise. Not for proof. Just... for the space.

He looks around the chapel—not for her, but for the echo she left behind. The sea glass. Now the sketch. Two offerings, unannounced, each left not as declarations, but as small, open silences. She had entrusted them to the room—not to him. And somehow, that makes them feel more personal.

It occurs to Julian that this is how *he* has always treated the chapel—not as a project to finish, but as a place to leave things behind. Thoughts. Memory. Absence. The ache of unfinished grief.

Maybe that's what drew her here, too.

Not the architecture. Not the restoration.

But the way the space holds you without asking anything in return.

Julian still doesn't touch the sketch. Not out of reverence—but alignment. It doesn't need to be moved. It has already found its place.

He doesn't know if Sera came here to remember something—or to forget. He only knows that she came alone. And that, in itself, is a kind of trust.

He turns toward the nave again. The light has shifted. The candle by the window burns steadily now. In the flicker between stone and flame, presence and trace, something has been marked—not loudly, not for anyone else to see, but just enough for the room to keep.

And somehow, that's enough.

Toward

The candle still burned.

Its small flame danced in the window's draft, casting a long, softened shadow across the chapel floor. Julian hadn't moved in some time. He stood near the edge of the nave, hands at his sides, gaze unfixed—not lost, but suspended. As though waiting for the silence to say something back.

But no revelation came. No jolt of clarity. Just the steadiness of breath in a space that now held more than its own history.

He looked once more toward the sea glass in the frame. Then to the sketch resting unclaimed, unprotected. They did not feel like objects. They felt like *traces*. As if Sera had passed through this place not to be seen, but to be felt. And in her leaving, had pressed something soft but certain into the structure of the room.

Julian had spent months restoring the chapel, and years before that restoring other things—beams, barns, broken eaves, fractured lintels. He had thought of restoration as return. As careful reassembly. As the architecture of memory.

But now… he wasn't so sure.

The chapel no longer felt like something he was fixing. It felt like something he was listening to. Or building toward.

Not for a grant. Not for legacy.

Not even for her.

Just—toward.

Toward the direction she moved in when she thought no one noticed. Toward the questions she hadn't asked but left between them. Toward the part of himself that had never been named but felt strangely at rest when she stood nearby, saying nothing.

He didn't speak again.

Words would not clarify this. They would only crowd it.

Instead, he lit a second candle from the first. Set it beside the sketch, careful not to scorch the edge. The two flames bent slightly in opposite directions, then curved toward one another again.

Outside, the storm had long since passed. But inside, something was still shifting—quietly. Like ground softening beneath old roots. Like stone releasing its hold, just enough to allow new weight to settle.

Julian stayed a while longer.

Not to finish anything.

Only to remain in the direction he now knew how to face.

Chapter 10

Things We Don't Fix

The chairs are hard in the way public chairs are always hard—narrow-backed, fabric scuffed, once maroon but now dulled into institutional anonymity. A metal rack of coffee cups rattles in the corner as someone restocks sugar packets. The air is warm, but not inviting—just the kind of stagnant, overhead-heated discomfort that makes your body long for motion even when you must sit still.

Wintermere's municipal hall isn't built for beauty. It's built for process. Fluorescent light flickers softly at one end of the room, haloing the projector screen that no one is looking at. Someone shifts in their seat. Another flips through a printed agenda without really seeing it. The same dull carpet. The same hopeful initiatives typed in sans serif and stapled into folders that will be forgotten by next week.

The meeting has already gone long, and everyone knows it. The modernization plan has passed committee. Just one more vote. Just a formality.

Sera sits in the third row, not quite in the center. She wears a charcoal blazer over an ivory blouse—practical, composed, the kind of clothing meant to signal neutrality. Her hands rest on a legal pad she hasn't written on. A capped pen lies across the lines like punctuation to a silence she hadn't planned to speak into.

She was told she'd be asked to sign later. Just observe for now. Support the final vote. No conflict expected. No voices raised. And certainly not hers.

Outside, the remnants of the storm still cling to the gutters and sidewalks, the smell of rain lifting from the town's brick and loam like a faint echo. It's the kind of evening where nothing should shift.

But something does.

A heat she hadn't noticed begins to rise at the base of her throat. Not the heat of nerves—she's managed plenty of public forums before—but the heat of friction. Of something being quietly *rubbed raw* beneath the surface. Not by anyone in the room, exactly. But by the language.

Bullet points.

PowerPoint.

Progress.

Terms she once wielded with pride now sit too comfortably on the tongues of others.

It's not opposition that unnerves her. It's how easily she might become complicit by nodding.

She glances down at the page before her. Typed notes. Project phases. Milestones. All correct.

All just slightly… wrong.

There's a phrase in her mind she can't trace the origin of, but it rises now:

"Not everything broken should be fixed. And not everything whole should be changed."

She isn't sure if Julian ever said it. Or if it's just something the chapel taught her by standing still.

Across the room, someone coughs. A motion is made. A second offered.

Her pen rolls gently off the pad and taps the floor, a soft clatter swallowed quickly by the room.

And just like that, something inside her—small, precise, almost surgical—begins to shift.

She draws in a breath, steady but unfamiliar.

And speaks.

The Break in Script

She hadn't planned to speak.

The role had been clear—observe, align, support. Smile when necessary. Offer a measured word afterward, perhaps, when the vote had passed and the tone had lifted. Say something useful, maybe even optimistic. Something that kept the machinery of process oiled and moving.

But there it was—that internal catch. A splinter, emotional more than logical. The kind that doesn't sting at first, but presses in over time, refusing to be ignored.

Across the room, someone reads from a typed statement. Something about community alignment, growth models, future readiness. The language is polished, precise. Sera knows the cadence well—she's used it, taught it, edited it into shape for others.

And yet, tonight, it lands wrong. Like a key turned in the

wrong lock.

Her throat tightens—not with panic, but with something slower. More deliberate. The sensation of having words form inside her that do not seek permission. Not from the committee. Not from her colleagues. Not even from herself.

She clears her throat. Once.

Not loudly—but not to herself, either. Enough to still the nearby shuffle of papers. Enough for the front table to glance up.

It isn't a rehearsed decision. It isn't even rebellion. The words come the way breath escapes when held too long—not dramatic, not strategic, just necessary.

And then, before she fully realizes it's her voice at all, she says:

"Some of this will harm what makes this place this place."

No emphasis. No apology. Not even a preamble. Just a clean, unadorned sentence. Spoken to the room. Not shouted. But unmistakably public. The kind of sentence that doesn't seek debate, only recognition.

The words hang in the room like smoke in still air. Not thick, not urgent. Just *present.*

For a breath, no one reacts.

Then a rustle—barely audible, but she hears it. The man to her left exhales through his nose, the way some do when holding back a scoff. Another flips her folder closed with a touch too much care, the gesture pretending to be casual.

It's not open opposition. It's something subtler.

The betrayal of professionalism.

That unspoken compact—say what supports the shared narrative, or say nothing at all—has been quietly broken. And she has broken it.

In a single sentence, her footing has shifted. Not publicly, not yet. But internally, she feels the tremor. The slight fray at the edge of her credibility. That sense that the woman who just spoke might be *less useful* now. Less trusted. Less included.

She doesn't look down. Doesn't apologize. But she feels it.

The old reflex—the one that wants to amend, soften, redirect—begins to rise.

But then the door opens.

The Arrival

She doesn't look down. Doesn't amend. But her body hums with that old reflex—the one that wants to smooth edges, to make discomfort more palatable.

And just as it starts to rise—

The door opens.

Not with drama. Not with warning. Just the quiet give of wood and hinge and presence.

Julian steps inside.

No umbrella. No paper in hand. Just him—shoulders damp, collar turned, carrying that same unhurried gravity as if he's crossed from a different world. One with no agenda. No minutes to approve.

He doesn't scan the room. Doesn't assess who's speaking or what's been said.

He already knows.

He moves along the edge—never intrusive, never uncertain—and stops a few feet behind her.

Not beside. Not in front.

Behind.

He doesn't speak. Doesn't nod. Doesn't gesture.

He stands.

Still. Steady.

And that changes everything.

The room continues as it had. A throat clears. A pen taps. A chair squeaks faintly. No one gasps or stares or claps.

But Sera knows.

She feels the shift—not external, but internal. The anchoring of something in her chest that had begun to unmoor.

He hasn't come to rescue her.

He's come to witness.

And there, in that silence, she understands:

She is not being defended.

She is being *stood with*.

The Edge of Risk

The meeting resumes, though Sera barely registers the motion. Someone proposes a minor amendment—language around "preservation integration"—the kind of phrase designed to sound like compromise but mean nothing at all. Another member murmurs support. It's seconded before the words fully land.

Votes will be counted. A document will be approved. The process, like water, flows around obstacles with practiced ease.

But Sera doesn't move. She doesn't lean forward. Doesn't fidget or nod.

She feels the cost arriving—not loudly, not instantly, but slowly. Like hairline fractures spidering through a pane of glass. The kind of damage you don't notice until you catch the light just right and realize the whole surface has changed.

Her standing has shifted. Not on the agenda. Not in the vote. But in the air between people.

There's a price to speaking outside the script, especially when you've helped write the script. Especially when your usefulness has always depended on a certain... fit. Measured. Professional. Persuasive.

She's spent years learning how to thread difficult truths into acceptable language. How to soften resistance with strategy. How to hold a room without unsettling it. But what left her mouth tonight wasn't shaped for safety.

It was shaped for truth.

And now, the reflex rises again—urge to apologize, to recalibrate, to approach the lead chair afterward and say, "I only meant…" But she knows how that goes. The moment she softens it, she undoes it.

Her hands remain still in her lap. But her pulse hasn't slowed. It's not adrenaline. It's awareness.

And then there's Julian.

She still doesn't look at him. She doesn't have to. His presence behind her is not performative. It isn't strategy. He didn't come to shift the room. He came to hold it steady.

To hold her steady.

No rescue. No validation. Just *solidarity without spectacle.*

And that's more disruptive than any speech she could have given.

What Remains

The meeting adjourns. Papers shuffle. Chairs scrape. A few hands are shaken with more form than warmth. Someone offers her a vague smile on the way out—the kind that covers distance, not bridges it.

Julian has already gone. She didn't see him leave. Didn't hear his boots cross tile. But the space behind her feels lighter now, like something certain has passed through and gone quietly.

Back in her room, she doesn't turn on the lights right away. The quiet is welcome—not empty, but uninsistent. She opens a bottle of red wine, pours a single glass, and leaves it on the table untouched for a long while.

There's no music playing. No need to fill the space.

She thinks about all the times she's managed a room—crafted a line, pivoted mid-question, salvaged a misstep with polish. It used to feel like strength.

But tonight, strength revealed itself differently.

It wasn't in her words. It was in what followed them. Not applause. Not validation. Just... presence.

Someone who entered not to shield her, but simply to stand where no one else had.

She didn't ask for it.

He didn't ask permission.

She stands by the small window overlooking the street and watches as the last of the night folds inward. There's no triumph here. No ruin either. Just the quiet, settled knowledge that something changed—and she was awake for it.

She doesn't know what this is between them—this wordless architecture forming in the pauses between actions.

But she knows what it isn't:

It isn't fragile.

It isn't ornamental.

And it isn't over.

The Reconstruction

The next morning, Sera returns to her work—on paper, at least. She answers emails with measured tone, reviews grant language, marks edits on architectural renderings. The mechanics of process resume. From the outside, nothing appears different.

But inside, something is.

It isn't defiance. It's not some brave new resolve. It's subtler than that—an adjustment in foundation. Like a support beam slightly realigned. Quietly. Permanently.

She walks the chapel perimeter that afternoon, not as a planner, not as a negotiator. Just as someone trying to understand what can be preserved without being embalmed. She watches how the light pools beneath the east eave, how the grass thickens at the back slope, how the salt wind wears differently on stone than on paint.

Her gaze lingers on the lintel Julian once touched.

She doesn't call him. Doesn't seek him out. But she feels the trace of his presence in the space. Not as memory. As pressure. Gentle, quiet pressure—like a hand not holding, but steadying.

She thinks about how often we try to fix what was never meant to be perfect.

How sometimes, the most faithful kind of restoration isn't repair.

It's accompaniment.

Chapter 11

The Language of Stillness

The wind wasn't cruel. Just persistent. It moved in long, unfinished phrases—never howling, never stopping. Just there. As if reminding the world of something it had once promised to carry. The tide pulled at the hem of the shoreline like a friend leaving too soon—tugging, pausing, then slipping back again. In the hush between waves, Wintermere's coast breathed in slow, fog-filtered silence.

It was the kind of morning that didn't ask for conversation.

Sera had set out alone. No destination in mind—just motion. The sort that asked nothing of her but attention. Her boots pressed damp impressions into the sand, the sea to her left, the cliffs to her right. It was a rhythm she didn't think herself into—only one she followed.

And then—he was there.

She rounded a slight bend in the trail near the overlook, where the path narrowed just enough to catch the breeze more directly. Julian was already standing there, a few paces off the footpath, just beyond the weathered fence that once marked the town's old boundary. Facing the water. Still.

No surprise crossed his face when he turned slightly. As if he'd known she might appear—not by appointment, not by design. Just by the shape of the day.

He didn't wave. Didn't speak. Only stepped back onto the path, falling into step beside her.

No greeting was exchanged. But the silence between them changed—slightly. Not filled. Not broken. Just acknowledged.

They walked without plan. Without the subtle calculations that often crowd two people trying to determine what this is. They walked like people who'd already shared something—though neither would have said what.

Sera walked slightly ahead for a while, then beside him. Then not quite. Their steps weren't mirrored, but they began to meet in rhythm—heel and toe, drift and pause. A quiet cadence, made not by choice, but recognition.

Julian wore the same salt-worn coat. Its sleeves pushed up just enough to expose the curve of his wrist, the shape of hands that had rebuilt things. He carried nothing. No tools. No bag. Just himself. As if today, witnessing was enough.

Sera didn't ask why he was there.

But when she saw him ahead, already waiting—not looking for her, but not surprised either—something in her unclenched. Not relief, exactly. Not expectation.

Something older than either.

Behind them, Wintermere moved at its usual tempo—coffee brewed behind fogged windows, shutters lifted, a dog barking once and then forgotten. Ahead, the ocean kept folding itself inward and outward, asking nothing in return.

Some silences close a room. Others widen it.

This one did neither.

It simply held.

And together—without speaking, without deciding—they stepped into it.

The Fragment

They reached the point where the path narrowed—where low grasses curled around the edges of the cliff and a scatter of stone interrupted the otherwise smooth trail. Julian slowed.

Sera didn't look over. But she heard the shift in his step. The slight catch in breath.

And then—he spoke.

"The chapel…"

He paused, as if the word itself held too much. Or not enough.

"It belonged to my grandfather."

Sera kept walking, but her eyes moved to him now—not insistently. Just listening.

"He waited there for someone," Julian said, his voice low, almost threadbare. "Years, I think. Maybe decades."

She didn't ask who.

He wasn't offering a story. Not in the way people usually do. This wasn't a performance. It was a fragment—found, turned over, and handed to her without decoration.

Julian stepped up onto a flat stone, pausing to let the ocean come into full view. The wind tugged gently at the edge of his coat. He squinted into the horizon, then spoke again—almost to the sea itself:

"He died still waiting."

Silence. Not for effect, but because some things don't need more than that.

"Some silences don't end," he added quietly. "They just settle into stone."

Sera felt the words find her—slow, deliberate, like the tide working its way around a rock.

She didn't offer comfort.

Didn't reach for a response.

There are moments when understanding asks nothing loud of us—only presence.

Julian glanced sideways—just once—and she met his eyes. Not with pity. Not surprise. Just… a kind of recognition.

The stillness in him, so often mistaken for aloofness, was something else entirely.

It was grief, held long enough to become architecture. A refusal to collapse.

They stood for a moment like that.

Not frozen. Just still.

The wind moved past them. The ocean continued its rhythmic argument with the shore. And behind them, the rest of the world—plans, noise, decisions—waited.

Here, in this moment, something else was speaking.

And they were both listening.

They resumed walking.

Not because the moment had ended, but because it had been heard.

The path opened slightly as they moved on—less narrow now, winding closer to the bluff's edge. Wind pressed softly at their backs. The ocean below surged and withdrew, speaking in a language neither had tried to translate.

Words had done enough. For now.

Sera tucked her hands into the folds of her coat. Not to shield against cold, but as a kind of tether. Something about Julian's voice—its worn edge, the way he let silence do most of the carrying—had settled under her skin. Not unsettling. Not warming. Just *present*.

They didn't speak again for a long stretch. And the silence between them shifted shape—not absence, not awkwardness.

It became a rhythm.

Seagulls called overhead, circling once before disappearing toward the dunes. He didn't look up.

She didn't need to.

There was something architectural about the way he moved—unhurried, solid, like each step had been etched in advance by some older part of him.

It wasn't performance.

It wasn't retreat.

It was reverence, she thought.

Julian kept his gaze ahead, but something in the set of his shoulders had softened. As if the telling—not dramatic, not explained, just offered—had emptied a small, hidden vessel inside him. Not entirely. But just enough to shift the weight.

Sera watched—not directly, but through proximity. Like reading the margin notes of a book rather than the text. His presence wasn't loud. But it was undeniable.

There's a kind of knowing, she thought, that doesn't arrive through answers.

It arrives through pace.

Through noticing what someone doesn't say.

And honoring it.

They rounded a bend where the sky widened, the brush falling away on either side. The ocean stretched vast and unpunctuated before them. And for a moment, it was hard to tell whether the hush between them came from inside—or from the sea itself.

Still they walked.

Not side by side, but close enough to feel the space narrowing.

Not by force.

But by quiet recognition.

The Almost-Touch

The trail narrowed again near a patch of low brush, where windswept branches leaned into the path as if eavesdropping.

They stepped closer without thinking.

It wasn't calculation. It wasn't choreography. Just the simple geometry of space.

And in that narrowing, it happened—brief, imperceptible to anyone but them.

Their sleeves brushed.

Wool against canvas. Barely contact.

But enough.

Enough to register. Enough to hold.

Neither drew back. Neither acknowledged it.

No glance. No word. Not even a pause in stride.

But the air shifted.

Not outwardly.

Inside.

Like the weight of a memory stirred by scent. Or a photograph glimpsed for only a second but never quite forgotten.

That kind of shift.

Sera felt it first as a flicker—not adrenaline, not tension. Something smaller. Quieter. Like a room she hadn't entered in years suddenly lit from within.

Julian didn't react. Not visibly. But the rhythm of his step changed—half a beat slower, as if allowing the moment to make space inside him.

And then the distance returned.

Not rejection.

Just… room.

Room to let the contact mean what it meant.

No more. No less.

There's a kind of intimacy, Sera thought, that doesn't require pursuit.

It asks nothing but presence.

They kept walking, the brush behind them, the moment already fading in form—but not in feeling.

Some touches don't announce themselves.

They leave no mark.

Only awareness.

And that is enough to change the shape of silence.

What Isn't Spoken

They reached the overlook just as the clouds thinned—silver strands drawn back to reveal a hush of pale sky. Below, the sea folded inward and back again, waves pulling in deliberate, measured swells. There was no drama in it. No crashing. Only return.

Julian stopped near the edge. Not too close. Just where the rock curved slightly inward, like a gesture of welcome.

Sera joined him, her breath visible now in the cooler air. She didn't speak. Neither did he.

But that was the language here.

Not avoidance. Not hesitation.

Just presence, held open.

The kind that doesn't fill silence to ease discomfort—but lets it breathe.

They stood like that—side by side, not touching, not looking directly. Watching the horizon.

It was the kind of view that didn't offer answers.

But it made the questions gentler.

Julian shifted his weight. A small motion. Then, without turning, he said:

"I don't know if he ever believed she'd return. My grandfather."

Sera waited. The words were slow, formed carefully.

"But he sat there. Same bench. Same hour. Every week."

He didn't say what that meant. Whether it was love or ritual or stubbornness. Whether it gave him peace or tore at him slowly. Maybe he didn't know.

Sera didn't ask.

Some stories aren't ready to be named.

She glanced sideways—not fully turning, just enough to catch the line of his profile. The stillness in him. The restraint that wasn't coldness, but care.

She wondered what it was like to carry that kind of waiting.

To build a chapel in its echo.

"I used to think stillness was avoidance," she said, softly.

"Like if I stopped moving, something in me would collapse."

Julian said nothing, but she could feel him listening.

"It's different here," she added. "With you."

The words weren't dramatic. They weren't meant to be. They just slipped out the way truth sometimes does—unadorned, unexpected.

And still, he didn't answer.

But his hand, resting at his side, stilled.

A quiet stillness. Not bracing. Not tense.

Just aware.

They stood like that until the sky dimmed further and the path behind them cooled in shade.

No promise was made.

No confession offered.

But something in the air—unseen, unspoken—held.

Not the start of something. Not the end.

Just a moment suspended—wide enough for two.

Gwen Observes

Later that morning, the fog still clung to the windows of *Mariner's Rest*. Sera sat near the corner, alone, her coat still damp at the sleeves from the sea air.

Julian had peeled away quietly after the overlook. No goodbye. No pause for meaning. Just a nod—barely a movement—before stepping off the path toward the chapel road. She hadn't followed. It hadn't felt like a moment meant for prolonging. Only for holding.

Now, here, she sat with a mug of plain coffee cupped in her hands. She hadn't ordered it. Gwen had simply placed it in front of her, warm and steady. The mug's heat pressed faintly into her palms, but she hadn't sipped. Not yet.

The café moved gently around her—chairs scooting across the floor, plates clinking in the dish bin, the hum of conversation low but unbothered. Jane moved behind the counter, fussing with the card reader, while Gwen moved through the space with her usual quiet authority.

She approached the table without ceremony, refilled a small carafe at her hip, and topped off Sera's coffee without asking.

Then, almost as if speaking to the air between them, Gwen said, "You two are like something left to steep."

Sera looked up. Brow slightly raised—not offended, just caught in the gentle surprise of being seen.

Gwen gave a half-smile. "Quiet, but strong. Hard to tell where it starts. Or what it's becoming."

There was no teasing in her tone. No insinuation, no agenda. Just a truth placed softly—like a folded napkin beside a plate. Uncomplicated. Undemanding.

Sera exhaled a small laugh through her nose. Not amused—just found. Her fingers traced the rim of the mug.

"We're just... working," she said.

Gwen tilted her head. Not in disbelief, not in agreement. Just receiving.

"Most worthwhile things are," she replied.

And that was all.

No advice. No theories. No clever follow-up. Just the grace of something shared and left alone.

Sera didn't move for a while after Gwen walked away. The mug remained warm. The sketchpad stayed closed. But her pen was in hand—uncapped, resting between her fingers.

Outside, the fog began to lift. Not all at once.

Just enough to see the outline of the sea beginning to return.

Chapter 12

Unmarked Blueprints

T he sound of graphite on paper is different from ink. Softer. Less decisive. It doesn't etch—it whispers.

Sera noticed that about a week ago. Or maybe longer. Time had blurred at the edges. Not lost, but loosened. Like ribbon unwinding slowly from a spool.

She no longer opened her laptop first thing in the morning. Instead, she reached for the mechanical pencil that had somehow made its way back into her bag. It wasn't deliberate. It was reflex. As though her hand remembered something her mind hadn't given permission to recall.

There were still documents to draft. Proposals to annotate. Measurements to double-check. She hadn't abandoned the project—at least not on paper. But her tools were changing.

Ink was for certainty. Ink sealed. Ink declared.

Pencil... wondered.

She sat by the window at the inn's breakfast room most mornings now. Same table. Same angle of light. The others—town officials, visiting engineers, a grant consultant who spoke too quickly—came and went with their routines intact. But Sera lingered.

The town hadn't changed. Not in any sweeping way. But she had started to see things she hadn't marked before.

The way the morning sun settled on the second-floor shutters above the hardware store, washing them in pale gold before fading. The cracked mosaic tiles outside the old pharmacy—someone's careful handiwork from decades ago, still holding together, still trying. The worn path behind the library that curved unnecessarily, but beautifully, as if leading nowhere in particular but insisting the journey matter anyway.

None of these things appeared in her diagrams.

But they had begun to show up in her sketches.

She didn't call them that—not yet. Sketching implied intention. This felt more like... noticing.

It wasn't rebellion. She wasn't resisting the plan. She just wasn't rushing to fix anything anymore.

The old reflex—the one that had shaped cities and calendars and Sera herself—still tugged at her when she wasn't looking. But now, more often than not, she let it pass.

There were no new drawings in the official binder that week. But three folded pages, smudged with graphite and margin notes, lived quietly in the back of her journal.

Unnumbered. Undated. Unmarked.

But not lost.

And each one, in its own way, began with a line that didn't know where it would end.

The Shift

The revisions came slower now.

Not because she was less focused. In truth, Sera's attention had rarely been sharper. But it had changed direction—tilted slightly, like light through a clouded window. Still bright. Still warm. Just no longer aimed at conclusions.

She found herself sitting longer before she marked a change. Hovering. Holding her pencil above a section of the map for minutes, sometimes more, without drawing anything at all. Her fingers would move—lightly, barely noticeable—along the paper's edge, tracing the faint indentations from earlier drafts.

In meetings, she spoke less. Not from doubt, but from caution. She was starting to understand that solutions too quickly offered were often only rehearsals—echoes of other towns, other templates. Wintermere wasn't echoing back. It was watching. Waiting.

There was something in the way people paused before they spoke here. How decisions took the long road—through conversation, through history, through silence. She'd called it inefficiency once. Now, she wasn't so sure. Maybe it was reverence.

Sera began walking the town not just for movement, but for proximity.

She lingered at the post office steps longer than she used to. Noticed how residents greeted the clerk by name, and how she replied with facts not just about mail, but about gardens, anniversaries, a cousin's return. On Wednesdays, Sera sat near the small park fountain, sketchpad unopened in her lap, listening to the afternoon rhythms of children calling out rules to games they hadn't invented yet.

It wasn't research.

It was something else. Something slower. More porous.

Her changes to the modernization plan had become tentative—suggestions rather than directives. She placed question marks in margins where once she would have placed arrows. She stared at a note that read "possible green space expansion?" for three days before realizing it had already happened—just not by her hand. A patch behind the chapel had grown wild with herbs and low-lying flowers. No one had landscaped it, and no one seemed to mind.

She stopped trying to correct it.

She started drawing it instead.

When her supervisor asked for the status update, she sent what was expected—progress reports, adjusted budgets, renderings that met the original criteria.

But none of them felt like the town anymore.

They looked like blueprints. But they didn't sound like Wintermere.

And for the first time in her career, that mattered.

She couldn't explain the change—not to herself, not in words. But she could feel it settle into her. Not like a decision, but like an ache easing.

Not everything broken needed fixing.

And not everything unfinished needed to be rushed toward completion.

Some things needed space to become.

Even cities. Even people.

Especially people.

The shift didn't announce itself. But others noticed before Sera acknowledged it aloud.

The first signal came in the form of a forwarded email.

Subject: *Final Overlay, Revised Proposal – URGENT*

There was no hostility in the message. Just concern wrapped in the polite cadence of expectation. A reminder that timelines were slipping. That something had changed in her submission pattern. That clarity—her brand—was starting to fray.

She didn't open it right away.

Later, when she did, she reread her own last set of annotations and found them foreign. Not wrong—just disconnected from how she now saw the place.

The next came as a check-in call from someone two rungs above her—one of those phone numbers that rarely lights up unless there's a boardroom tone attached.

"Hey, just touching base," came the bright voice on the other end. "We're noticing a few deviations from the benchmark phrasing. The alignments are… softer than usual. Is there a strategy behind that?"

Sera sat in her room, feet tucked under her, pad in lap. She had been sketching the overhang of the library entrance— capturing the part where ivy climbed, almost unnoticed, into the cracks of the original brick.

"I think," she replied slowly, "I'm seeing some new layers we didn't consider."

A pause. Not long enough to be awkward—but not short enough to be supportive.

"Well," the voice offered, "just be sure we don't lose the through-line. We've worked hard to get them on board. Let's not confuse the message now."

Sera nodded, though the person couldn't see her. "Right. Understood."

But she didn't feel misunderstood.

She felt translated. Mis-translated. Turned into a version of herself that no longer fit quite right.

By the end of the week, three emails bore the same phrase in different forms: *Just circling back…*

And in her drafts folder sat a dozen replies she never sent. Not out of avoidance—but because she couldn't yet answer the questions being asked of her.

Questions like:

What is the goal of these revisions?

Are you re-aligning the proposed community zones intentionally?

Do you need support adjusting back to the initial vision?

She read those lines over again and felt, viscerally, how much of her career had been shaped by the ability to answer those kinds of questions instantly.

And now—she didn't want to.

She didn't want to correct what she hadn't misread. Didn't want to defend what she hadn't destroyed. Didn't want to fix what she no longer saw as broken.

Instead, she watched the way sunlight moved across Wintermere's uneven curbs. Listened to the wind touch the old fire station's bell tower. Studied the tilt of people's hats when they walked headlong into the morning fog.

The town was not disordered.

It was simply alive.

And suddenly, the plans she had once drawn with such authority began to feel like overlays that blurred something truer beneath.

The noticing wasn't just coming from above.

It was coming from within.

Coffee with Ruth

Ruth wasn't on the payroll. She didn't hold a title, didn't send memos, and wouldn't be caught dead in a planning committee meeting. But in Wintermere, her authority required none of those things. She didn't design structures—she anchored them. Her presence, like the seawall, had simply always been there. Steady. Weathered. Respected.

Sera had seen her around for weeks now—leaning against her bookshop doorframe as if guarding the town's unwritten history. The shop, tucked between the post office and an old hardware store, bore no signage beyond a hand-painted name fading into the wood. Inside, it sold books no one asked for but everyone ended up reading—titles that seemed irrelevant until they weren't. Poetry anthologies, field guides to clouds, a biography of a lighthouse keeper who'd never left the coast. All shelved without order, yet never out of place.

Ruth also stocked stationery older than the state highway system and once organized a Thursday night poetry circle that turned into a town-wide pie tasting. No one could quite explain how that happened, but it was still referenced like local lore.

Her gray hair was always twisted up—neatly, efficiently, as though she'd done it a thousand times without once looking in a mirror. And while her voice never raised, it always landed. Even her silences seemed to lean forward.

Sera hadn't planned to run into her that morning. She was on her way to sketch the bandstand—pencil tucked behind her ear, satchel slung loose. But Ruth had already seen her coming, and with a nod that doubled as a summons, had gestured toward the small table outside *Mariner's Rest*.

"Sit," Ruth had said simply. No question. No hesitation. Just a soft command in a voice that didn't entertain refusal.
Before Sera could reply, a chipped ceramic mug appeared across the table. The tea inside was dark, fragrant, and steaming, already steeped—just like the comment that followed.

"You need something warm," Ruth added, folding her hands as if the rest of the conversation was merely a matter of waiting.

And somehow, Sera sat.

Not because she needed the tea.

But because something in Ruth's presence made it impossible not to.

They didn't speak right away. Ruth tore her muffin into uneven halves. Sera sipped and tried not to notice that her own shoulders had relaxed for the first time that day.

"You've changed how you look at the town," Ruth said eventually. Not accusatory. Just observant.

Sera blinked, not sure if it was meant as a compliment or a warning.

Ruth didn't clarify. "It used to be lines and zones. Future this, modern that. And now… it looks like you're trying to see what's already here."

Sera didn't respond.

"You drew the bandstand yesterday," Ruth added. "I saw you. Penciling it like it might tell you something."

Sera gave a soft laugh, eyes dropping to her cup. "Maybe I just needed the quiet."

"Quiet doesn't change your lines," Ruth said gently. "Curiosity does."

There was no edge in her tone. Just a kind of settled knowing that came from living long enough in one place to watch others arrive, reshape, and retreat.

"You've started looking at this place like someone who might stay," Ruth said after a moment. "Not just fix it and leave."

Sera didn't answer—not because she disagreed, but because something about the words clung too close. Like mist that finds its way beneath your collar and makes you pause, just long enough to feel changed.

They sat a few minutes longer. The tea cooled. The café hummed with low sounds—chairs moving, spoons against ceramic, a baby cooing somewhere in the back.

When Sera finally stood, Ruth didn't offer advice or parting wisdom. She just folded her napkin once, then said, "Keep drawing. Some answers come that way."

That evening, Sera passed the town bandstand again. The light was low, and no one lingered nearby. She pulled her sketchpad from her coat pocket, sat on the cold bench, and traced the railing slowly. No measurements. No overlays.

Just pencil. And time.

The Quiet Defiance

She didn't answer the emails.

They'd stacked up throughout the afternoon—some marked "high priority," others disguised as gentle nudges. Subject lines filled with words like *alignment, timelines, clarity needed.* Messages that sounded like support but carried the weight of something else—expectation, unease, the beginning of doubt.

She read them. Every one.

And then she closed her laptop. Not in frustration, not in protest—just in finality.

It was still early, the kind of early that no longer belonged to the workday but hadn't quite turned into evening. The sky was low with cloud and quiet color, and the streets held that in-between stillness only small towns seem to know. Where shops begin to pull in their signs, and porch lights flicker on without anyone needing to be reminded.

Sera didn't change her clothes.

She didn't gather a bag, or bring her sketchbook, or check the weather.

She simply stepped out of the inn and began walking.

It wasn't a purposeful walk. Not one of those brisk, urban paces filled with mission. This was something softer. More internal. The kind of movement that didn't know its destination, only that it needed motion.

The chapel path wasn't the most direct route to anything. But her feet found it anyway.

As she turned down the gravel lane, she noticed that her breath had slowed. That her shoulders had uncurled. That she wasn't thinking about overlay files or municipal design parameters. She wasn't calculating.

She was… feeling.

The wind met her gently, not cold, but awake. It tousled her hair and carried the faint scent of brine and cedar. The chapel rose slowly into view—still, familiar, unmarred by urgency. Its stones catching the last of the light like they remembered how.

She paused at the low wall, running her hand across its surface. Rough, warm. As if it had been holding the day's sun and wasn't ready to let it go.

No one was there.

Not Julian. Not any of the volunteers. No committee members taking final measurements or snapping site photos.

Just the chapel.

And her.

She stepped inside—not out of habit, not even out of longing. Simply because the open door asked nothing of her.

The room received her like it always had. Quietly. Without judgment.

She stood for a long moment in the center aisle, then drifted toward the back bench—the one he had once fixed alone, the one she never sat in before. This time, she did.

She didn't cry. She didn't speak.

But something inside her shifted—something small, unceremonious, like the creak of an old floorboard reminding you that you're not alone.

She leaned back and looked toward the ceiling. Not for answers. Not even for clarity.

Only to be held by the shape of stillness.

By the possibility that not every change needed permission.

That some acts of defiance come quiet.

Not against someone. But for something.

That night, she didn't return to her inbox.

She didn't return to her drawings.

She stayed until the light dimmed, until the air cooled, until her own thoughts softened into something that felt like beginning again.

And when she finally walked back down the path, it was with no plan. No declaration.

Only the knowledge that something had been reclaimed.

Not from the town.

But from herself.

Chapter 13

The Room She Never Entered

Light moved differently through the chapel that day. It didn't pour. It crept.

Thin ribbons, angled and soft-edged, filtered in through the high windowpanes—quiet as breath, steady as memory. Dust, caught mid-air, floated not with weight but with waiting. The whole space seemed suspended, like it had been paused between heartbeats.

Julian stood near the side door. Not the main entrance, not the rear passage used by the volunteers. A narrow threshold, barely noticeable behind one of the old wooden sconces—an architectural afterthought to most. But his hand rested on it now, fingers brushing the aged brass handle, not turning it. Just... remembering it was there.

Sera had entered before him that morning. She'd paused to look upward—the sun catching the upper arches—and then moved toward the nave with that same quiet ease she carried in recent weeks. She didn't speak. Neither did he. But their silences had begun to take shape—rounder, more companionable.

When she turned and caught him watching the side door, she didn't question it. She only tilted her head, almost imperceptibly. Not an invitation. Not a request. Just acknowledgment.

Julian took another breath—low, unhurried. Then he reached into the pocket of his coat. The key was small, almost too small to matter. Not ornate. Not hidden in any special box. It had lived for years on a hook behind his father's tool bench, mistaken once for a drawer lock, left alone when it fit nothing else.

But Julian knew where it belonged.

And what it opened.

And what it didn't.

He didn't look at her as he turned it in the lock.

The sound was quiet, a dry click that broke no peace.

Then the door swung open, slow on unhurried hinges.

The air behind it was cooler. Still.

It smelled of wood, dust, and a faint trace of something older—like paper sealed in cloth, like oil once poured for light.

Julian stepped aside.

He didn't speak.

Didn't explain.

Sera stood at the threshold, one hand brushing the frame, as if needing to feel the grain of it before entering. She glanced once at him, and he gave the faintest of nods.

Then, silently, she stepped into the room she never knew existed.

And something in the chapel shifted—barely, like the weight of withheld memory exhaled through a stone wall.

The door eased shut behind them without a click—just the soft thud of wood meeting wood.

Inside, the air held a stillness that didn't feel abandoned. It felt kept. As though silence had been deliberately placed here and tended to like something sacred.

Julian didn't speak. He didn't move ahead or linger behind. He simply stood beside her, his hand brushing the frame as if reacquainting himself with the threshold.

The room wasn't large, but it expanded in a way that made size irrelevant. One tall, arched window caught the morning light and fractured it slightly, casting a thin shard of brightness across the floor. Dust hung in its path, suspended like time trying to remember how to settle.

Sera's eyes adjusted slowly. Not because of the light, but because of the feeling. This wasn't a space meant for public things. It wasn't part of the tour, wasn't diagrammed on any layout.

It was private. Maybe not secret. But something smaller than either word could fully hold.

A wooden desk stood in the corner, old and patient. Not pristine—this wasn't a preserved exhibit—but clearly cared for. A cloth, folded once, lay neatly across the top, and beside it, a framed icon rested against the wall. The image was almost worn through: a woman in muted robes, halo faint, expression caught somewhere between sorrow and surrender.

Beneath the window, a bench waited. The grain of the wood had grown pale where years of light had touched it.

Sera stepped forward, her boots nearly silent on the warped floorboards. And then she saw the paper.

A child's drawing.

Folded once and held in place by a small, smooth stone.

She didn't reach for it. Not yet. But she let her eyes take it in—the simple lines, the thick wax strokes, the way the sun crowded the upper corner as if joy didn't know boundaries. A chapel, clearly. A bench. Two figures drawn apart, but turned slightly toward each other. Not holding hands, not facing fully— just… aware.

Julian remained still. Not watching her, not studying her reaction. Just present.

When he finally spoke, it was quieter than the room required.

"I didn't know it was here. Not until after he died."

She turned, barely. Enough to acknowledge. Enough to let him continue if he wished.

"I found the key in a jar of nails," he said, the trace of a dry laugh in his throat. "Like it had been hiding in plain sight all that time."

Sera nodded. She didn't ask whose drawing it was. She didn't ask why he brought her here.

Some rooms aren't for questions.

They're for keeping what hasn't been spoken.

Julian moved to the window. Placed his hand on the sill. The light caught the edge of his coat, softening him. He didn't offer history or explanation. Only this:

"No one's seen this in years."

And somehow, it was enough.

Holding Stillness

Sera didn't move toward the desk.

She didn't take a photograph. Didn't sketch. Didn't catalog the space in her mind like she once might have.

She just stood there.

Her arms rested loosely at her sides. Not crossed, not poised for movement. Simply at rest. Her gaze wandered—not in survey, but in presence. She noticed the faint fray of the cloth on the desk's corner. The worn slope of the icon's frame where hands, long gone, might have once touched. The faint curve in the windowpane that made the outside world appear softer, as if even light had to bow slightly to enter this room.

Time didn't stop. But it stopped mattering.

This wasn't a room for chronology. It was for… continuation. Not in the linear sense. But in the way memory endures—not always recalled, but always waiting.

She stepped once toward the bench. Sat carefully, as if asking permission. The wood held a slight give beneath her, shaped by other bodies who'd once rested here. She folded her hands loosely in her lap and exhaled—one of those releases that comes from someplace deeper than breath.

Julian hadn't spoken again. He stood quietly near the door, not guarding it, not retreating. Just allowing. His presence was like the room itself—unobtrusive, but anchoring.

Sera let her eyes fall again on the drawing. She didn't lean in. She didn't try to interpret the figures or assign meaning. She simply let the image exist. It was enough that it had been placed there. Enough that it had lasted.

No analysis. No speech. No mapping of symbols onto stories.

Just stillness.

And not the performative kind that seeks to be seen as composed.

The kind that arrives when something deeper inside finally says, *stop*.

She didn't know how long they remained like that. Five minutes. Fifteen. Maybe more.

But when she finally stood, she didn't speak either.

She gave the room a glance that was not farewell, but acknowledgment. Then met Julian's eyes for the briefest second—not in search of explanation, not to ask what it all meant—but to say, wordlessly: *I understand that I won't understand everything. And that's alright.*

He gave a slight nod. Nothing more.

They left the way they came—in silence. But not in absence.

Something had been offered.

And something, just as gently, had been received.

The Walk Back

Sera stepped outside first, the chapel door easing closed behind her with a softened groan. Julian hadn't followed immediately. He hadn't said anything more. And she hadn't asked him to.

The air felt thinner out here—brighter, somehow, though the sky hadn't cleared. Clouds still hung like unwrung linen, casting diffused light across the gravel lane. But the weight of the room, its held breath, still clung to her.

She walked without hurry. No path marked this stretch beyond habit, yet her steps knew where to go.

The drawing remained in her mind. Not just the content—the sun crowding the edge, the two figures bent slightly toward each other—but the lines themselves. The angle of the chapel roof, too steep. The window placed too low. But there was affection in its inaccuracy. Not decoration, but remembrance.

She couldn't say why it caught at her so.

It wasn't just the innocence of it. Or the quiet intimacy of the two drawn figures. It was something about the colors. The untrained weight of the crayon strokes. The fact that the stone holding it down had clearly been chosen with care, not at random. She could feel, absurdly, the small hand that might've placed it. A child's hand. Or—

She paused.

Could it have been Julian's?

The question arrived uninvited. But once there, it refused to leave. He hadn't said. Hadn't implied. But something in the way he'd stood there—quiet, unpossessive, but also strangely… proximate.

It wouldn't be a boast, if it were his. It wouldn't even be nostalgia. It would be something else entirely.

An offering.

She rounded the corner by the post office and glanced briefly toward the shopfronts. The windows were catching their usual light again. Life resumed its gentle clockwork—doors opening, wind chimes clinking, a boy chasing a ball too close to the curb. But the room still pressed at her like a thumbprint in soft wax.

By the time she reached the inn, her steps had slowed.

She didn't go inside right away. Instead, she sat on the stone bench beneath the crooked oak—pencil still in her coat pocket, sketchpad untouched.

And she stared for a long while at nothing in particular.

Just letting the image live a little longer.

Not asking what it meant.

Only wondering who had drawn it.

And why it had been left to wait so long.

Julian Alone Later That Night

The light had long gone. Only the faint spill from the chapel's front sconces offered any guidance as Julian stepped back inside, alone.

He hadn't turned on the main fixtures. Letting the dark remain mostly intact felt more honest somehow. The old wood accepted his return without sound. Only the low creak of one familiar board marked his passage as he crossed the nave and slipped once more through the narrow side door.

The room felt smaller now. Not because of the dark, but because it had been shared. Something about another presence, even briefly, had nudged the space into a different shape.

He let the door rest half-open behind him.

The desk waited, same as always. The icon. The bench. The stillness.

And the drawing.

Julian approached slowly. Not like one returning to a memory, but like someone stepping back into a part of himself left untouched too long.

He picked up the smooth stone—thumb tracing its roundness once—and set it gently beside the paper. Then he lifted the drawing. For the first time, he didn't just glance. He looked.

Really looked.

The thick lines. The absurdly high sun. The crooked angles of a building that still somehow held.

Two figures, not quite meeting.

He remembered the wax crayons. The way they'd snapped too easily under pressure. The way he'd once tried to fix something with color because no one could explain how to fix it with words.

He didn't remember drawing *this*. Not precisely. But he knew the feeling it came from.

He knew the hand.

Julian leaned the paper upright, resting it gently against the base of the icon. Not quite an altar. Not quite a shrine. Just a place where it wouldn't be hidden anymore.

And then he sat.

The bench creaked slightly under his weight, but settled. So did he.

Outside, a fog had begun to drift in from the coast. The kind that made edges blur and time loosen.

He didn't pray. Not exactly. But he stayed.

And after a long silence, he whispered:

"Thank you."

Not loudly. Not with certainty.

Just softly. Toward the quiet.

Toward whatever part of the past had left something behind, not for keeping—but for returning to.

He closed his eyes.

Chapter 14

Outside the Frame

Evening pressed gently across the stones of the chapel, as if the light itself were reluctant to leave. The sun had begun its slow withdrawal behind the western hills, but it did not vanish. Instead, it lingered—soft, golden, low—stretching itself into corners where time moved differently.

The air was still, not breathless but aware. A single leaf spun once in the drift and settled near the base of the chapel wall, its landing soundless.

In the trees nearby, wind traced through the canopy like a memory recalled but not yet named. It didn't rattle or rush. It simply passed—carrying with it the weight of something unsaid. Along the narrow path that curled away from the town, the footfalls of the day had faded. No voices rose, no laughter spilled. The town hadn't silenced—it had settled. As if Wintermere, too, understood the value of a pause.

Somewhere, faint and behind shuttered glass, a radio played the end of a song no one would remember. A screen door clicked closed two streets over. A dog barked once. Then stillness again.

Time did not stop. But it hovered.

The world, in its ordinary rhythm, had made room for something. Not dramatic. Not loud. Just possible.

And in that held breath of light and quiet, two figures moved slowly toward each other—not summoned, not scripted. Simply drawn by a gravity neither had fully acknowledged, but both had begun to trust.

Through the Slowness

They walked without intention, without destination, their steps falling into a rhythm that neither set nor resisted. The path ahead wasn't chosen—it unfolded beneath them, a thread through the trees, narrow and uneven, stitched with patches of light and the broken shadows of branches above.

Julian kept his hands in his coat pockets, but not deeply. His fingers curled slightly at the edges, brushing the fabric as if uncertain whether to remain hidden. The chapel's scent— woodsmoke, salt, old dust—still lingered faintly on his coat. It mixed now with the dusk air and something else—something just behind them, or between.

Sera matched his pace without trying to. She wasn't counting steps, but she noticed how hers landed just after his, and how that closeness didn't jar her. It steadied. Not in the way plans steadied her, but like a metronome set to a softer beat—something alive rather than engineered.

Their arms occasionally brushed, lightly, unintentionally at first. The first time it happened, Julian pulled in slightly—not from discomfort, but from instinct. The second time, he didn't. By the third, the space between them no longer felt neutral. It was charged. Not electric. Not dramatic. Just… deliberate. Even when no one reached.

He noticed her breath catch once. Just the smallest hitch. He didn't look at her, didn't ask, didn't name it—but it landed in him. And in that silent landing came a memory, half-formed and uninvited: a time, long before this, when he had noticed the same faltering in someone else—and turned away from it. Out of caution. Out of a desire not to presume. And because he hadn't known how to hold something that trembled near him.

This time, he didn't turn. He didn't lean in, either. But he stayed close enough to feel it.

Sera, for her part, had stopped trying to translate her thoughts into language. Words rose—small, unfinished things— but none of them felt right. She wasn't afraid of breaking the silence with speech. She was afraid of reducing it. Some silences felt blank, dull, like an obligation or a withheld truth. But not this one. This silence moved. It curved and flexed around them. It made space for things she hadn't yet allowed herself to imagine.

She wanted to say something, and didn't. Not because she couldn't—but because anything she might say would feel smaller than the moment.

The sun was lower now, its angle cutting long gold slashes through the thinnest trees ahead. The path curved slightly to the right, leading them toward a grove she hadn't walked through before—not with him, not alone. But her feet didn't question it.

There was no rush. No clock chasing them. No audience. Just the rhythm of one step following another, and the quiet tether between their arms—not quite touching now, but never far.

He glanced once, briefly, not at her face but at her hands. She noticed. Said nothing. Let him look.

And in that look, in that step, in that nearness, something else stirred—something not quite nameable, not yet—but present.

It did not ask to be spoken. It asked only to be allowed.

A Place Beyond Planning

The trees began to thin.

The path spilled them into a small clearing just as the last of the light stretched wide. It wasn't a place they'd aimed for. Not a destination on a map. But it held the kind of accidental perfection that makes one believe in unseen design. There, the chapel was visible again—just its eastern corner and a sliver of stained glass catching the gold—framed by the darkening canopy above.

Neither of them pointed it out.

They slowed without discussing it, the way one might instinctively bow their head when entering a sacred place. Not from superstition. From recognition.

To their left, vines had climbed across a low stone wall, draping it in living lace. Just above, an arched growth of trees leaned toward each other, forming an accidental overhang—a hollow not built, but granted. Beneath it, the air was cooler, touched by earth and bark and something ancient in its patience.

Julian paused first, one foot resting slightly forward, his weight angled in, not fully planted. Sera followed his line of sight, but didn't speak.

She stepped beneath the overhang, her shoulder brushing a hanging strand of ivy. It clung to her sleeve for a breath, then let go.

For a moment, they stood there—not shoulder to shoulder, not face to face. Slightly askew. Aligned only in nearness.

A single leaf, small and mottled with early autumn blush, released from the canopy above and drifted between them. It twirled once, hovered like it couldn't decide, then dropped gently to the space between their feet. Neither bent to pick it up.

Sera's gaze tracked its fall, then lingered on it longer than the moment required. There was something comforting in the way it landed—unannounced, but whole.

Julian's attention stayed with her, just enough to catch the angle of her face in profile. The way the edge of her mouth softened—not into a smile, but into something unguarded. The quiet of her expression matched the quiet in the clearing. Present. Without defense.

He felt no urgency. But he felt something. A presence. A draw. Not toward action, but awareness. There was no need to fill the air, no gap demanding speech. What lived between them now wasn't absence. It was permission.

The kind that isn't granted out loud.

Behind them, the path still glowed faintly, the day not entirely gone. But ahead—this space, this hollow framed by ivy and stone and air held still—this felt apart from time.

And in it, they stood, unworried by what came next.

Not because they were sure of each other. But because the moment itself was enough.

What Readies the Heart

A breeze stirred—slight, almost apologetic.

It swept down from the ridge and moved through the overhang like a breath released after long holding. The ivy rustled faintly above them, the vines brushing one another like soft cloths in a darkened room. It wasn't cold, but the air held a crispness, a subtle edge that hinted the season was changing.

Sera's hair lifted at the ends, caught by the wind. A few strands brushed across her cheek.

Julian saw it happen—the way her fingers started to rise but didn't. The gesture half-formed, then faltered. And before she could finish it, his hand moved—only slightly—then stopped.

He didn't touch her. But the impulse was real. The desire to tuck that one strand behind her ear, not possessively, not even protectively—but as a way of saying: *I see you. I want to offer something simple.*

But he let it go. His hand hovered mid-thought, then fell back to his side.

She hadn't turned to look, but she had felt the shift. That brief pulse in the space beside her. It caught in her chest—not as disappointment, but as something else: confirmation. That the silence wasn't indifference. That his nearness wasn't accident.

Behind them, the chapel bell gave a faint creak—wind, not intention. It didn't ring. Just swayed slightly in its frame, iron against iron, a dry hinge muttering in the dusk.

Down the hill, from the town's edge, a dog barked. Once. Then again.

A window closed somewhere in the distance, the sound of a wooden latch catching. A child's laughter carried briefly, then stopped. The ordinary life of the village continued, indifferent to the weight of the clearing.

And maybe that made it better.

They weren't in a storybook. No orchestration or script. Just two people who had walked long enough in the direction of silence that they now found themselves inside a different kind of knowing.

Julian shifted his weight slightly—forward, not away. His shoulder came almost level with hers now, though he still left a fraction of space between them. The kind that could be crossed easily—or not at all.

Sera breathed in slowly. She didn't close her eyes. Instead, she looked straight ahead, through the opening in the trees, to where the chapel's upper window caught the last light. In the stained glass, a fractured shaft of amber bent across the sill like a finger marking a page mid-thought.

She spoke no words. Neither did he.

But inside her, something began to unclench. A loosening that had nothing to do with certainty—and everything to do with choice.

They didn't reach for each other. They didn't confess or explain.

They simply remained.

And it was enough.

Not because it filled the ache, but because it honored it.

Not because it solved the silence, but because it shared it.

And in that, something unfamiliar and sacred took shape— slowly, like light blooming in a place long hidden from the sun.

The Frame Left Behind

They moved again, almost at the same time.

No signal passed between them. No nod. No gentle touch.

Just a quiet mutual instinct that the stillness had done its part.

Julian stepped first, his boot brushing against a patch of moss that had gathered at the edge of the stone wall. The sound was soft, almost like fabric. Sera followed, her pace matching his once more, though the rhythm felt subtly different now—not faster, not slower, just fuller. As if the steps they took were no longer tracing an edge, but stepping into a shape not yet drawn.

Neither of them looked back.

The clearing remained behind them—untouched, unchanged in appearance. But something had shifted. Not in the trees. Not in the air. In the space between their two paths, now one.

As they passed the bend, a flicker of golden light flared briefly on the far chapel wall, catching the rough stone where the old mortar had started to crumble. It wasn't dramatic—a mere glint, a last exhale of the sun's retreat—but it found its place in the moment like punctuation at the end of a sentence not yet spoken.

Neither of them pointed it out. Neither needed to.

They didn't name what had happened between them. Not because they feared it—but because naming it might contain it. And some things—especially beginnings—are best left unbounded.

Behind them, the clearing held its quiet.

No footsteps marked the ground. No trace announced that two people had stood there on the verge of something.

If there were a frame, it would hold only the light.

Not their faces. Not their bodies. Just the hush of what almost became.

And if a camera had followed, it would have stopped just short of the turn—held its gaze on the empty clearing, on the leaf still resting between two parallel shadows. As if to say: *this is where something sacred chose to remain unseen.*

Outside the frame, they walked on.

Together. Unspoken.

But not unchanged.

Chapter 15

The Kiss

The last traces of light lay low across the landscape like a shawl pulled gently over tired shoulders. Not enough to see by, but enough to feel by. The trees no longer cast shadows. Instead, they became silhouettes—tall, unmoving figures standing witness to something they would not speak of.

The air had stilled. Not with finality, but with expectancy. The kind of quiet that no longer served as backdrop, but now carried its own substance. It was a presence. A pressure. A held breath stretched across the clearing, across the path, across the narrow space between two people who had not planned to stop, but had.

A single bird called out once from somewhere above them. A brief, uncertain note. Then silence again—as if even the bird had changed its mind.

The chapel no longer glowed. It stood hushed in the distance, just a darker shape against the darkening sky. Its lines softened. Its edges blurred. What remained was not the building but the memory of it—what it held, what it witnessed, what it waited for.

The path ahead faded into shadow.

But neither of them moved forward.

There was no wind now. No motion in the trees. Just the sound of their breath—quiet, steady, human—and the faint, rhythmic creak of one of Julian's boots pressing into the earth, then shifting.

They weren't holding hands. They weren't even speaking. But something between them had already turned.

Not the kind of turn one feels in conversation, or in the flicker of a glance. This was the slower kind. The kind that builds across days. Across near-misses and almost-gestures. Across silence shared too often to be called coincidence.

In this moment, time didn't stop. It simply stepped aside.

And in its place: a hush so complete, so charged, that even stillness became language.

Where It Lands

They had stopped.

Not by intention, not by coordination. There was no landmark to pause for, no bench, no boundary. The path simply fell away beneath them, replaced by a patch of open earth pressed flat by years of passing feet. A place no different than any other— except that it caught their momentum and held it.

Julian noticed first—not the stillness, but the shift. The way their feet had aligned, almost exactly. How his shoulder had turned slightly inward, not to face her, but to receive her. It was the way someone turns to light without knowing they've done it.

Sera didn't speak. She let her gaze travel—not quickly, but slowly—from the outline of the trees, down the curve of the path, and then toward him.

She didn't look at his face right away. She looked at the space just beside it, the way one looks at a doorway before entering. Not with hesitation. With reverence.

When her eyes did find his, it wasn't sharp or expectant. There was no need for confrontation or clarity. Her expression was quiet, offering nothing scripted. It simply asked: *Are you here?* Not with her voice—but with the angle of her chin, the stillness in her breath, the way she didn't look away.

He didn't answer. Not out loud. Instead, his gaze moved downward—to her hands. They hung loosely at her sides, not fidgeting, not clasped. One finger traced the seam of her coat. The gesture was small, almost imperceptible, but it grounded her in the moment like a pin holds fabric to form.

Then he looked back up.

Their eyes met—not with urgency, but with weight. A long-held awareness, finally permitted to surface.

The space between them grew louder. Not in sound, but in feeling. A presence thick enough to change the air. They weren't touching. But the absence of touch now felt like its own form of contact. A language composed entirely of distance and direction.

Julian stepped slightly closer—not boldly, not hesitantly. Just enough.

She didn't move back. Her body answered him without effort. Not by leaning in, but by staying still.

The space between them changed shape. It stopped being absence. It became invitation.

Then, quietly, Sera lifted her chin—not dramatically, not as provocation. It was a gesture so subtle it could have been missed if one wasn't looking directly at her. But Julian saw it.

And he didn't fill the space.

He let the moment arrive.

Not as a decision. As a becoming.

The First Touch

The kiss arrived not with a gasp, not with a reach, but like a shift in temperature—barely perceptible at first, then unmistakable.

Julian leaned forward only slightly. His shoulders softened, not in surrender, but in care. Not in certainty, but in permission.

He didn't move fast, didn't close his eyes too soon. He watched her—watched the quiet in her, the steadiness, the way she didn't flinch or lean away.

And when their lips met, it wasn't hunger.

It was breath.

A touch so light it barely registered as contact, and yet everything else seemed to disappear into it. The trees, the chapel wall, the hard-packed earth beneath their shoes—all of it faded into backdrop, into texture, while the center of the world compressed into the space between their lips.

Their lips didn't move. They didn't explore, didn't press.

They simply met.

Like the way wind touches the back of the hand on a still day—soft, unasked for, yet unmistakably there. There was no tension in it. No claim. Only recognition. A whisper of something that had always been waiting behind the silence, behind the glances, behind the paths that brought them here.

For Sera, it was not the kiss itself that startled her. It was the stillness inside it. The way it made room for her. The way it didn't ask her to perform or explain.

For Julian, it wasn't about having kissed her. It was about having allowed himself to feel what it stirred.

And what it stirred was not certainty, but exposure.

They didn't close their eyes at the same time. Hers drifted shut first. His followed only near the end—as if reluctant to lose sight of her in the moment he most needed to remember.

And then, just like that, it passed.

They didn't linger.

There was no second kiss. No inhale of sudden need. Just the soft pullback of presence returning to itself.

Their foreheads didn't touch.

Their hands remained at their sides.

But something between them had been named—without being spoken—and it would not go unnamed again.

Time, which had stepped aside only moments earlier, now resumed its place.

But it did not rush in.

It deepened. Like light soaking into a well-worn page. Like memory settling into the body before thought can catch it.

The Withdrawal

He pulled back.

Not sharply. Not as a break.

It was more like the soft retreat of a wave after it touches the shore—not from regret, but from knowing its own limits.

Julian's head dipped slightly as he stepped back, no more than half a pace. His eyes remained low—not in shame exactly, but in effort. As if meeting her gaze would tip something over, would undo whatever balance the stillness had managed to hold.

His hands stayed at his sides, open, unhidden. He wasn't

leaving. But something inside him had already begun to edge away.

"I wasn't ready to feel this," he said.

The words came low, almost as if spoken to the ground.

Not dramatic. Not confessional. More like a line of thought escaping before it could be reconsidered. His voice didn't tremble, but it caught—on something not yet named. Not her. Not the kiss. But what the kiss had stirred awake.

He still hadn't looked at her.

Instead, his eyes hovered somewhere just below her collarbone, near the place where her coat folded at the chest. A fixed point—like a foothold in a moment he didn't know how to stand in.

Sera didn't move. Didn't reach for him. Her breath was steady, but inside she felt the shift—the way his presence had loosened, as if some part of him had already turned and walked back into the quiet he came from.

She didn't chase him with questions.

He didn't offer further explanation.

But between them now was a third thing—not the kiss, not the words, but the silence that came after. And it was not empty. It was full. Of feeling, of what might have followed, of what had been almost given.

Julian finally lifted his eyes—just enough to meet hers.

And in that gaze, there was no apology. Only fear. Not of her—but of the truth he couldn't yet live fully inside.

What She Doesn't Ask For

She didn't interrupt the silence.

That was its own kind of answer.

Julian's words had landed—*I wasn't ready to feel this*—and where someone else might have asked why, or what changed, or what now, Sera simply received them. Not out of coldness, not out of confusion—but out of something deeper. Something she had learned in her own silences: that not all truths require handling.

Some simply need room.

So she stood still. One hand loosely curled, thumb grazing her knuckle. Her gaze remained with his—not demanding, not wavering. Just present.

And in her quiet, Julian felt something unexpected: not shame, but permission. The kind that doesn't urge you forward, but also doesn't push you away. It holds space around your fear without naming it weakness.

She nodded once.

Small. Intentional.

The kind of nod that says: *I heard you. You don't owe me more than what you've just given.*

He looked at her a moment longer, then exhaled—not a release, not relief. Just breath. Just the act of remaining in her presence, even now that he had pulled back.

Still, neither of them moved.

The path was open in both directions. Behind them, the chapel stones had already grown dim. Ahead, the woods thickened with the fading light.

She could have said something. She had the words.

"It's okay."

"I wasn't ready either."

"We can take our time."

But all of them felt too small, too early, too much.

So instead, she gave him the only answer that matched his honesty:

Silence, held without resistance.

Not silence that withdraws—but silence that stays.

And that silence wrapped around both of them now. A second skin. A softened veil between what was felt and what was acted on.

It didn't erase the kiss. It didn't dissolve the moment.

It simply preserved it.

The Turning Away

Eventually, the body must move, even if the heart lingers.

Sera shifted first. Not a step, just her shoulders—squaring slightly, as if gathering herself. She glanced toward the path again, this time not to avoid him, but to acknowledge what still lay ahead. The walk back. The night coming. The quiet that would follow, even in her own room.

Julian's posture mirrored hers, though he didn't know it. He, too, had turned slightly—just enough to feel the pull of direction. Not away from her. But away from the edge of something vast and unnamed.

They didn't say goodbye.

They didn't make plans.

There was no brush of fingers, no backward glance.

But as they began to move—first slowly, then with quiet rhythm—there was something in the way their footsteps stayed near. Not in unison, but not far apart either. Like the echo of something they hadn't quite begun, but hadn't ended, either.

When they reached the bend, the clearing fell out of view.

The light had faded completely now. Only the faintest silver-blue traced the horizon. And in that hush, in that deep twilight, they walked into the next silence together—not holding hands, not speaking—but known.

And the kiss remained—not a question, not a promise. Just a presence.

Like a candle left unlit in a room you return to, again and again.

Chapter 16

The Distance Between Hands

The rain returned without drama. Not the theatrical kind—no thunder, no heavy drops pounding against roofs or glass. Just a soft, persistent drizzle. The kind that sinks into things. Into the seams of jackets, the spaces between cobblestones, the quiet rooms of people who don't say much aloud anymore.

In Wintermere, windows dulled. Light no longer spilled through them—it stayed behind the fogged panes, caught in its own uncertainty.

Even the sea looked subdued. Not angry. Just distant.

Somewhere near the square, a door creaked open, then shut again with the slow inevitability of something not meant to draw notice. Footsteps echoed against tile, the kind that belonged to people not in a rush, not entirely present either.

Sera moved through her mornings deliberately now. Her shoes made soft, high squeaks against the old corridors of Town Hall. She didn't apologize for the sound. She didn't even register it anymore.

In the café, Jane began to wipe the same section of counter over and over without realizing. Gwen hummed to herself behind the storeroom curtain—a low, tuneless sound that drifted out like a memory one doesn't intend to speak.

Across town, Julian passed the chapel on foot. He didn't enter. He didn't pause. But he slowed—just slightly—when the old wooden door came into view. Not enough to be noticed by anyone watching casually, but enough for the chapel to notice him. Enough for the memory of her presence inside it to surface— unbidden, unfinished.

Elsewhere, Sera crossed the square in the same coat she had worn the night of the kiss. Her gait was steady, her posture unchanged, but something in the way she held her satchel closer to her side made people pause. A touch of guardedness. Of inwardness. Not sorrow—but something close.

They were seen—both of them. Still present in Wintermere. Still part of its quiet rhythm. But never together now, and that was what made people look twice.

They had not been lovers—not in any public sense. No announcements, no gestures. But their nearness had once carried a weight that others had felt. A gravitational pull that had gathered around them like mist—never spoken, never asked for, but noticed.

Now that weight was missing.

And in its absence, a different kind of stillness had settled in.

People noticed. Gwen, wiping down a counter. Ruth, shelving a book more slowly than usual. Even Father Anselm noticed.

He had served Wintermere's small parish for nearly twenty years, a man of sparse words and deep silences.

He stepped out into the drizzle, coat collar raised, his gaze pausing just a few seconds too long in the direction of the chapel steps—where someone used to wait, and now didn't.

No one asked.

Not because they didn't care.

But because in a place like Wintermere, you learn to respect the sacredness of distance. You learn that some wounds are carried not in bruises or words, but in the way a person walks down a familiar street without scanning the crowd.

What do you say to the ones who still look the same—but now move like someone else is missing?

Nothing.

You simply notice.

You make room.

And you let the silence say what would only be made smaller by questions.

Rain beaded on the glass, on the metal, on the shoulders of coats left hanging too long by the door.

Letters were received and left unopened. Sketches remained folded. Tools sat out but untouched. Stories that might've begun paused themselves mid-sentence—unwritten not from lack of meaning, but because too much meaning had gathered at once.

The world didn't break.

It blurred.

And in that soft blur, between rooms and glances, paths and passing, something ached—not from distance alone, but from the unbearable nearness of what hadn't fully arrived.

Sera began writing in pen again.

Not for efficiency. Not for permanence.

But for the illusion of certainty—of lines that couldn't be taken back once drawn.

Pencil had once been her quiet indulgence, a medium for sketching the possible. Erasable, suggestive, forgiving. Now, forgiveness felt indulgent. She craved definition.

Her handwriting changed slightly in ink.

It grew sharper at the edges, less patient in its loops. She no longer lingered on letters the way she once did. There was no softness in the curves of her R's, no lift in the tail of her Y's. The pages bore her sentences like blueprints stamped and approved, even if no one had asked for them.

She rewrote the chapel proposal three times. Not because it needed revision, but because her hands needed somewhere to go. Structure became a kind of shield. Margins were filled with precisely boxed annotations. Timelines, materials, phased implementation schedules. Precision as protection.

She no longer used post-its. Instead, everything was transcribed into a single black planner, where nothing would flutter out or remain unaccounted for. When Jane passed her a coffee at *Mariner's Rest*, she thanked her too crisply. When Ruth offered to walk her home one afternoon, Sera said, "No need," in a tone so measured it felt rehearsed.

Order, after all, asked nothing of her heart.

At Town Hall, she stayed later than needed—filing, editing, reorganizing. She erased old names from her whiteboard and replaced them with budget figures and acronyms. She was praised for her focus. Someone even joked that her productivity had doubled. She smiled, not because it was true, but because it helped maintain the shape of a self she could still hold in public.

At night, she returned to her room and sat on the floor with her legs tucked beneath her like a child. Not to meditate, not to cry—just to be still in a way that didn't require interpretation.

The sketch remained folded inside her journal. She'd tucked it there weeks ago, almost without thinking. A page drawn loosely in pencil: lines with no names, no destination. It carried the shape of something begun in silence. She never looked at it now, but she kept it close, like a note she wasn't ready to read aloud.

Instead, she made lists.

Emails to return.

Supplies to restock for a project whose future no longer felt hers to shape.

She planned without passion. Lived without mess.

And if some part of her ached in the quiet of routine, she did not name it.

To name it would be to let it breathe.

And she feared what it might become, if allowed.

Tools Without Purpose

Julian found himself moving without intention.

He sharpened wood he didn't plan to carve. Sanded corners already smooth. Sorted screws by type and length, then resorted them again, as if some new logic might emerge from the repetition.

The bench inside the chapel sat half-finished, untouched for days. A length of oak leaned against the far wall, marked but uncut. He walked past it each morning, touched its grain with the back of his knuckles, but never lifted the chisel. The tools remained where he'd last placed them—square, true, waiting.

He couldn't remember the last time he swept the floor properly, though he still brushed away the larger pieces of dust and wood shavings out of habit.

It wasn't neglect.

It was inertia.

Some days he stood at the chapel doorway and watched the light shift across the pews. The windows filtered the late autumn sun in a way that made everything look touched by time—softened, slowed. The silence inside was not oppressive, but it had changed. It no longer felt like a refuge. It echoed now.

He still lit a candle some mornings.

Still filled the small basin with fresh water from the well. But it felt more like tending a space he'd been asked to leave gently. As if the room knew what had shifted before he did.

At home, tools remained laid out on the counter. Unused brushes. A graphite pencil worn to its final inch. A broken measuring tape he hadn't bothered to replace. He kept thinking he would—next week, or after finishing the bench. But the bench wasn't being finished. Not yet.

His hands, once steady with task, had begun to hesitate.

He washed dishes slowly. Repaired a jacket seam that wasn't torn. Tightened the handle on a drawer that hadn't come loose. It was movement for the sake of motion. Work that wouldn't ask for meaning.

When he saw Sera crossing the square one morning—shoulders slightly hunched against the cold, eyes fixed just beyond the horizon—he turned before she saw him.

He told himself it was out of respect.

But later, standing in the workshop doorway, he wondered if it was also fear.

What if she looked and saw a man who didn't know how to fix what had cracked quietly between them?

What if she didn't look at all?

He pressed his thumb along the spine of the chapel blueprints, rolled them again, and slid them back into their tube.

It made no sound.

But something in him folded with it.

Shared Spaces, Missed Moments

One morning, just before the rain turned heavier, Julian stepped into *Mariner's Rest*.

The café was quiet, caught between breakfast and late arrivals. Jane handed him a paper cup without a word. He nodded once, paid in cash, and left before the song playing overhead reached its second verse.

An hour later, Sera arrived—hood damp, shoulders drawn close. She chose a table near the window, the same one Julian had passed on his way out.

She didn't drink right away. Just traced the rim of her mug in slow circles, her thumb pausing at a chipped edge.

She didn't know why that table had drawn her. Only that it felt like the place where something might have been.

Neither knew the other had been there.

And Jane, watching from behind the counter, said nothing.

Later that week, Sera walked the coastal path just after sunrise. The fog hadn't lifted, and the sky was a dull sheet of gray.

She moved without direction, stepping around puddles without really seeing them.

That evening, Julian followed the same stretch—his boot print landing beside the faded echo of hers.

He paused once near the bend in the path, looked out to sea, then kept walking.

If either had turned back—just once—they might have seen the other.

Two outlines, dim through mist, close enough to touch.

But they didn't.

And so the ache continued—shaped not by anger or absence, but by almosts.

The kind that press into you softly, until you can't quite tell where the missing begins.

When Almost Hurts

They crossed paths twice in one week.

Once by the seawall—he turned down the western trail just moments before she rounded the bend. She saw only the blur of a coat, the back of a head, the fading trace of footsteps dampened by rain.

The second time, near the café steps, they came within twelve feet of each other. Julian exited *Mariner's Rest* holding a folded paper bag, Sera approaching from the opposite side of the street. A delivery truck pulled forward just then, its diesel cough breaking the silence. By the time it passed, neither was in the other's direct line of sight.

Or so they pretended.

Each time, one of them looked down.

Each time, one of them turned a second too soon.

It wasn't avoidance. Not in the active sense.

It was something far softer—and far more brutal. A hesitation born from the ache of proximity without belonging.

They were too near to be strangers.

Too uncertain to be anything else.

That nearness—unresolved—began to hollow them out. It wasn't the silence that hurt. It was what the silence couldn't contain anymore. The possibility that what had formed between them might not survive its own quiet.

Sera caught herself walking the long way around the square to avoid the chapel. Then the next day, she walked straight toward it and passed by without glancing up.

Julian sanded a length of oak for an arch brace he didn't need, working the grain until his wrist ached. He stopped when he realized he wasn't building anything anymore—just erasing time.

Neither of them was angry.

Not at each other. Not even at themselves.

But the ache kept growing, not from what had happened, but from what hadn't.

The kiss had opened something. But it hadn't landed.

And now, every glance at a doorway, every brush of shared space, was a kind of emotional recoil.

Like standing too close to a threshold you're not ready to cross again, but unable to walk away from either.

They had grown skilled at navigating almosts.

Avoiding the places where memory gathered too thick, timing their routes unconsciously so footsteps would not overlap. But the cost of such precision was heavy. And quiet doesn't always mean peace.

Some nights, Sera sat at her desk with the pen poised above the page, not writing.

Some nights, Julian stood at the chapel's threshold and turned back without touching the door.

Not because they didn't care.

Because they didn't know how to approach what had once opened without unraveling.

And eventually, something inside her shifted.

Not loudly. Not completely.

But just enough to want to be seen again—not by everyone. Just by him.

The Pinecone

She woke before the sun. Not from restlessness, but something quieter—a steadiness beneath the ache.

There was no grand plan. No carefully written message. Just a small instinct that rose without noise:

Go.

Sera pulled on her coat, still faintly creased at the sleeves, and stepped into the early mist. The town hadn't yet stirred. Only the faint drip of rain from eaves, the soft rustle of leaves brushing one another in sleep.

She walked the familiar path to the chapel slowly, but not reluctantly.

Each step was a breath she didn't rush. Each corner she turned felt like crossing into a version of herself she hadn't quite abandoned.

In her pocket, she carried nothing but a pinecone—round,

dry, unbroken.

She had found it two days earlier on the wooded path behind Town Hall. It reminded her of something—not childhood, not poetry, just continuity. A small shape the world had offered without demand.

When she reached the chapel steps, she didn't go inside.

She paused at the entry, touched the railing once, and crouched—placing the pinecone just to the right of the door, nestled where the stone met earth.

No note. No initials. Just presence.

She stood again, her breath visible in the cool air.

For a moment, she looked up toward the window where the light used to spill when he worked late. It was dark now. Still.

Then she turned and left.

The offering wasn't about rekindling.

It was about being seen again—if not fully, then enough to remind him that some silences aren't endings. They're invitations. Or at least the beginning of one.

The same morning, a little after sunrise, Julian stepped out behind his house with no intention. Just movement.

He didn't dress for work—just pulled on a threadbare sweater and boots he hadn't waterproofed in years. His hands were raw from sanding, though he hadn't touched the bench in days.

He didn't know where he was going until he was already headed there.

The town was barely stirring. A truck engine idled somewhere distant, but Wintermere still belonged to fog and footsteps for now. When he reached the chapel, he stopped halfway up the path.

There it was.

The pinecone.

Not fallen. Placed.

Tucked gently, deliberately, where no wind could have left it. He didn't touch it at first.

Just stood. Looked. Let the stillness settle between them—him and the object that wasn't just an object.

It said nothing. But he heard it.

A small quiet message: I haven't left. Not entirely.

And something softened in him—not enough to name. Not enough to move.

But enough to notice that the ache had shifted. Slightly.

He bent down, lifted the pinecone, turned it once in his palm.

It didn't answer anything.

But it asked something.

He stood again, stepped inside the chapel without really thinking.

Then, after a long moment, he sat. Not to work. Not to plan. Just to be in the space she had once entered with light in her breath.

When he rose again, the pinecone was still in his hand.

The Burned Note

Back inside, the chapel felt different—not brighter, not warmer, but aware.

Like something had been acknowledged in the silence. Like a space had been made.

Julian didn't light the lamps. He let the gray seep in through the high windows, let the shadows gather in the corners where tools waited but weren't reached for.

He placed the pinecone gently on the sill beside the window that faced the sea.

Then sat at the narrow workbench where he'd once drafted joinery plans and restoration notes. The pages were still there, curled slightly from weeks of neglect.

He pulled one free. Turned it over. Picked up a pencil. Then put it down.

He reached for a pen.

The words came quickly—far too quickly for something he hadn't let himself feel fully.

I'm still here.

That was all. Four words. Enough to crack something inside him.

He stared at the ink. His fingers trembled—not dramatically, just enough to blur the shape of his own handwriting in his mind.

It felt both true and cowardly. A message meant for no one unless delivered. A presence declared and then hidden again.

He sat there for nearly ten minutes, reading the same line over and over, as though trying to will it into meaning, or safety.

Then he stood. Took the page outside.

The wind had quieted. The drizzle, stopped.

He touched a match to the corner of the paper and watched the flame curl into the words slowly. The ink resisted for a second, then gave in.

The page folded into itself as it burned—bright, then soft, then gone.

Julian didn't drop the ashes. He let them fall where they would. Some clung to his coat. One piece floated up, hovered, then landed gently on the sill beside the pinecone.

He didn't brush it away.

He just stood there, quiet as the stone around him, with his hands in his pockets and something unspeakable resting in his chest—not as burden, but as truth.

Chapter 17

The Reassignment

It arrived without fanfare. Just an envelope among others. White. Sealed. Thin enough to suggest something short, but weighted enough to matter.

The return address—the **Office of Community & Regional Development**, several towns inland—felt sterile even in print. She had been there once for a quarterly meeting: a building where the walls smelled faintly of toner and the hallways swallowed voices, as if even sound wasn't meant to linger.

She didn't open it right away.

She laid it on the counter. Made tea. Washed her hands. Let the kettle whistle longer than necessary.

When she finally slid her finger beneath the flap, the paper made a sound like something giving in.

Dear Ms. Linden,

In response to recent structural realignments and project scope considerations, we are initiating a reassignment of duties. You are hereby appointed Interim Regional Projects Liaison, effective immediately. Your cooperation in ensuring continuity during transition is appreciated.

No signature. Just a printed name beneath a title she didn't recognize.

There was no mention of Wintermere.

No acknowledgment of the work done. No gratitude, no regret.

Just appointment.

And expectation.

She read it twice.

The second time, slower—as though that might reveal a different subtext.

It didn't.

Her hands remained still.

Only the rise and fall of her breath shifted slightly, the way it does when the shape of something internal begins to bend without breaking.

No one had asked. No one had warned.

Only the rain outside spoke plainly, tracing downward paths along the window, soft and indifferent.

And Sera, standing alone in her room with the letter in her hand, understood that the distance between her and Wintermere had just been decided—not by failure, not by timing, but by someone else's version of what continuity looked like.

The paper didn't tremble in her grip.

But something inside her did

Boxes Meant to Close

Sera packed with the kind of precision that left no room for second thoughts.

Folders fit perfectly in boxes designed for documents. A thin roll of blueprints slid beside a lined notebook she hadn't opened in weeks. Bubble wrap cradled a stapler she'd never liked but used anyway.

She labeled everything—permanent marker in clean block letters:

ARCHIVE

REFERENCE – OLD BIDS

TO RETURN

There was no label for what lingered beneath words. No sticker for uncertainty. No checkbox for almost.

She didn't rush.

She moved in timed increments, pausing only to refill her tea or stare briefly out the window.

There was no music. No messages.

Only the sound of drawer rails sliding open and the soft scrape of cardboard edges.

It wasn't until her coat was buttoned and the last box was stacked neatly by the door that she remembered the pinecone.

Not remembered, exactly.

She had thought of it earlier—then pushed it away.

But now, with her keys in hand and the afternoon light thinning by degrees, she turned and left her room.

Not far.

Just a quiet walk back to the chapel.

The front doors were locked, but one side window was still cracked open for ventilation. She reached through, gently, her fingers brushing against the sill.

It was there.

Half-shadowed behind a dusty hymnal and a votive box. Right where he had placed it after finding it outside.

She hadn't known he'd kept it.

Hadn't planned to retrieve it.

And yet—here she was.

She cradled it in one hand as she returned to the office.

Set it down carefully on the edge of the desk.

Finished sealing the last envelope.

Then she stood still.

The pinecone fit easily in her palm.

Cool. Familiar. Unchanged.

She didn't hold it like a relic.

She held it like a thread—not a keepsake, but a tether.

Something to carry—not to dwell on, but to remind herself that what she'd felt was real.

That something once placed with intention could still matter, even after the space around it had emptied.

She slipped it into her coat pocket.

Zipped the coat.

Lifted the first box.

And didn't look back.

Drafts Without Recipients

She opened the laptop out of habit, not intention.

The screen glowed too brightly in the dim room. She adjusted the angle, then adjusted it again—stalling.

Her inbox was clean. Overly so.

Everything sorted, flagged, filed. The kind of order that only surfaces when something else inside is coming undone.

She clicked *Compose.*

Her fingers hovered, then typed:

You should know…

She stared at the words for several seconds.

Backspaced.

Tried again:

If I had more time…

Deleted.

The cursor blinked. Quiet. Expectant.

It didn't rush her. But it didn't leave either.

She leaned back. Let her hands fall to her lap.

Her chest felt hollow in a way that couldn't be named—like all the unsaid things were gathering just beneath her collarbone, asking to be translated. But she didn't have the language. Not for this.

She exhaled. Closed the screen.

There would be no message.

No subject line. No salutation.

Some words weren't meant to arrive.

Some truths lived best in the space between intention and delivery.

And some messages, she realized, were written only to know they could be written at all.

She sat in the stillness a little longer, her reflection faint in the darkened glass.

Then she stood.

And walked away.

Order as Survival

At the regional office, everything was beige and boxy.

Desks too square. Chairs too firm. The walls buzzed faintly from overhead lights that never turned off.

Sera arrived on time, smiled when she was expected to, and kept her sentences short.

She answered questions with nods and mild affirmations. "Absolutely." "Understood." "No trouble at all."

Colleagues accepted her efficiency like a welcome breeze. No one asked how long she'd be staying. No one asked where she'd come from.

That suited her.

She reopened old files—project briefs from towns that blurred together.

Pinefield. Lark Hollow. Benning.

She copied whole paragraphs, inserted Wintermere's name like a placeholder, like a ghost.

As if by doing so, the town might linger a little longer on her screen, if nowhere else.

Each section clicked into place.

Stakeholder matrix. Timelines. Contractor notes.

Her fingers moved automatically.

It was easier when things fit into boxes.

When the work could be named, numbered, sent.

Then she reached the "Community Engagement" section.

Her cursor blinked.

The words on the screen didn't move.

She stared at the empty space reserved for signatures.

A soft line marked:

COMMUNITY PARTNER – NAME / DATE

Her hand hovered over the keyboard.

She thought of the sketch folded in her journal.

The bench no one sat on.

The silence at the chapel's door.

And beneath it all, she thought of the way Julian never asked her to stay—and how she had left anyway.

She didn't delete the line. She didn't fill it in, either.

She let it remain:

Open. Unclaimed.

A name not entered.

A space that still held weight.

Then she saved the file, closed the screen, and moved on.

Not Quite Gone

She returned once more to Town Hall—

"Just to collect a file," she told herself aloud, though she never quite specified which one.

The front doors gave way with their usual creak, but it sounded different now.

Less like a welcome, more like a memory turning over in its sleep.

The lights were dimmer than she remembered, though no bulbs had changed.

The air held a faint scent of dust and citrus cleaner. Familiar, but faded.

No one sat at the front desk. The cushion still held the faint imprint of someone who hadn't returned.

The plant near the window wilted slightly at one edge, untended.

No fresh mug on the counter. No offhand joke to fill the space between task and glance.

She stepped lightly, as if walking through a house not quite hers.

The storeroom door was closed. No shuffling behind it. No humming, no rustle of supplies.

Only the dull echo of her own footsteps, trailing longer than necessary down the hall.

She passed the meeting room without meaning to slow—but she did.

The door was cracked just enough to see the edge of the long table inside.

She remembered the night he stood behind her.

Not touching. Not speaking.

Only presence.

It had steadied her more than words ever could.

Now, the room held nothing but stillness.

The chairs were tucked in too neatly, as if no one had sat there in weeks.

The projector had been unplugged.

Even the air felt hesitant, like it was holding itself back.

Still, she lingered.

Her fingers brushed the edge of the doorframe, lightly. She didn't step inside.

Didn't need to.

Some rooms didn't need to be reentered to be remembered. Some moments stayed not because they were revisited, but because they had once held weight.

She stood a moment longer, then turned—not with urgency, but with the kind of quiet acknowledgment that comes only when something is not quite gone.

And never really will be.

A Room Left Unlocked

On her way out of town, Sera took the long way—past familiar turns, past the bench near the bakery where she once sat with half a thought toward staying longer.

The chapel stood in stillness.

Not waiting. Not abandoned. Just... present.

Its door was slightly ajar. A shift of wind could have done it, but it felt intentional—like a breath held open.

She didn't step inside.

But she moved closer.

Close enough for the scent of old wood and faint salt to rise. Close enough to see where the grain of the door had worn smooth near the edge—years of hands, moments of hesitation, quiet arrivals.

She reached out, her fingers resting lightly against the frame. Not to knock. Not to lean.

Just to feel something that hadn't asked anything of her.

The wood was cool.

She stood like that for a breath, maybe two.

Then she let her hand fall.

And walked on.

Through Glass

The taxi idled by the curb, engine low and indifferent.

Sera slid into the back seat without a word. The driver didn't ask where she was headed—just glanced in the mirror, then pulled away.

Wintermere blurred past the windows:

The edge of the square.

The bend in the road where fog liked to settle.

The café sign, half-lit even in daylight.

She didn't lean her head against the glass. Didn't cry.

But as they passed the chapel one final time, her eyes lifted—just once.

For a flicker of a second, she imagined him there.

Not standing in the doorway. Not chasing the car. Just inside, where the light slanted warm across the floor. Maybe sanding something. Maybe looking up, unsure why.

He wouldn't know she was leaving.

Not officially. Not directly.

But he'd feel it.

Somehow, he always had.

She didn't wave.

Didn't reach for anything.

She just watched the road unfold—and let Wintermere fade behind her, without ever fully letting go.

The Distance Between Assignment and Desire

The train moved steadily, indifferent to the choices that had placed her in seat 14B.

Sera sat with the folder open in her lap—her name printed cleanly at the top of each page, as if certainty could be typed into existence. She traced the headings with her eyes: *Community Assessment Priorities, Projected Engagement Metrics, Integration Timeline.* She uncapped a pen, circled a date, underlined a phrase. Not because it mattered yet, but because she had always believed in marking beginnings—even the kind that arrived without welcome.

Around her, the train whispered forward. Across the aisle, a man dozed with his blazer bunched behind his neck. The rhythm of the tracks offered no comfort, only motion.

She looked down again at the page—tried to absorb its language. But the words felt hollow. Measured. They carried direction, but no desire. Expectation, but no invitation. She could already see how it would unfold: templates copied, reports sent, calls answered. She would meet deadlines. Be efficient. Say "of course" when asked for more.

She turned the page. Made a small note in the margin. Closed the folder.

Then her hand drifted to her coat pocket—found the shape of the pinecone. Still there. Unspoken. Solid.

She didn't hold it.

But she felt the weight of it like something pressing faintly against her ribs, reminding her of a place where meaning had not come with instruction.

The coastline vanished somewhere between stations, swallowed by fog and inland trees. She glanced out the window just as the last stretch of water blurred from view.

Something caught in her chest—not grief exactly, but a kind of ache in the gut, sharp and low, as if her body had noticed the absence before her mind could name it. A quiet internal folding.

Her reflection hovered in the glass—half-lit, half-lost.

She hadn't chosen the reassignment.

But she had chosen not to fight it.

That, too, was a kind of surrender. One that didn't declare itself with tears or protest, but moved inward—taking up space beneath her collarbone, behind her ribs.

The train curved inland.

And with it, the version of her that might have stayed—might have tried—slipped further out of reach.

171

Chapter 18

Resignation

The hinges made no sound when he opened the chapel door, but the silence that followed felt heavier than any creak could have.

Julian stepped inside slowly, as if expecting the stillness to rearrange itself around him. It didn't.

No scent of morning coffee lingered. No paper edges curled where she'd once spread her notes. The chair she used to move slightly off-center remained pushed in, aligned too perfectly—as though no one had touched it in days.

He stood in the entryway for longer than he intended, keys still in hand, his eyes tracing corners for things that weren't there. The air was cooler than usual. Or maybe it only felt that way.

He moved toward the back, out of habit, not purpose. The floorboards accepted his weight without protest. Nothing shifted. Nothing offered welcome or resistance.

He touched the edge of the worktable lightly, then let his hand fall away.

Even the dust felt undisturbed.

It wasn't just that she was gone.

It was that the space had stopped expecting her.

Julian exhaled through his nose—soft, almost inaudible—and turned to leave.

He closed the door more slowly than he'd opened it. It didn't click shut; it just rested against the frame.

Outside, the wind moved through the trees without pattern.

Inside, the silence remained—but not the same as before.

It had taken on shape.

An outline of someone no longer there.

And somehow, that was louder than sound.

The Bench Completed

He had left it unfinished for days.

Not because it was difficult—he could've completed it in one afternoon—but because leaving it undone gave him a reason to stay a little longer. A pretense of usefulness. Something tangible to return to.

But now, the final sanding block sat in his hand.

He pressed it gently to the edge of the seat, moving in slow, even strokes. Not out of deliberation—out of quiet. Out of that strange instinct to treat silence with care, as if it might shatter.

The wood was soft beneath the grain.

Not new, but forgiving.

No carvings. No initials.

No dedications, plaques, or marks to remind anyone who had shaped it.

Just smooth surfaces. Angled legs. Balance.

It would hold weight without complaint.

When he finished, he ran his hand along the length of the

seat. Not to check for splinters—there were none—but to feel what care felt like when it no longer had a recipient.

He set it near where the altar had once been. Not centered, not off to the side.

Just... placed.

Not as a gesture. Not as a legacy.

As a finish.

The light through the chapel windows shifted slightly across the bench, catching the wood in muted tones—like a thing ready to be forgotten, but made to endure anyway.

Julian stood for a while, watching the bench hold its place in the room.

Then he turned away.

Not because he was done. But because the act of finishing no longer required staying.

The Drawing

He hadn't meant to open the drawer.

He was reaching for a chisel he'd misplaced, something routine. His hand tugged at the handle without thought, fingers smudged with sawdust. The drawer slid open a little stiffly—like it hadn't been touched in weeks. Because it hadn't.

And there it was. Folded once. Slightly off-center.

The sketch.

He knew it was hers the moment he saw the edge—the faint curl of the paper, the texture of the graphite smudge where a fingertip had once pressed too long. He didn't have to unfold it to see the lines. He already remembered them: the rough outlines of St. Avila's, its windows unfinished, its roof captured mid-thought.

A place drawn not for presentation, but to understand something. To feel it.

He let his hand hover above it.

His thumb brushed the corner, slow and deliberate. Not possession—just recognition.

For a moment, he considered opening it.

To look again. To remind himself of how she had seen the chapel—and maybe, just maybe, how she had seen him.

But he didn't.

Not because he didn't want to.

Because wanting didn't seem like enough anymore.

Some things, once unfolded, couldn't be returned to their former shape.

He eased the drawer shut. Softly.

As though the paper inside might feel it.

And then he stood there a little longer, hand resting lightly on the surface.

Not holding on. Not letting go.

Just... pausing.

Because some artifacts aren't meant to be used.

And some moments are clearest when left untouched.

Conversations That Stay Small

He walked to *Mariner's Rest* because it was what he did.

Not every day. Not at a set time. But enough that the habit had hardened into something like ritual.

The bell above the door still chimed. The scent of cinnamon and old wood lingered near the window booth, though the pastry case looked emptier than usual. Jane wasn't behind the counter. It was Gwen who nodded at him, wordlessly, and poured the tea without asking what kind.

He took his usual seat—third table from the back, where the sun hit for just a few minutes midmorning.

She joined him a few minutes later, sliding into the chair across without a word. No menu. No notepad. Just her own mug cupped between weathered hands.

They didn't talk right away.

Didn't need to.

He looked out the window, where the clouds had settled low and soft, like they were holding something back.

"She's gone then," Gwen said.

Not a question. Not quite a statement either. Just enough breath to give shape to the obvious.

He nodded.

"That letter came through," he offered, finally. "Reassignment. Interim liaison. Some title that doesn't mean much."

Gwen didn't nod. Didn't sigh. Just waited.

He traced the rim of his cup with one finger.

"She didn't say goodbye."

"She didn't have to," Gwen said gently.

He looked up, eyes tired but not surprised.

For a moment, they sat like that—two people suspended between the presence of words and the comfort of silence.

"She left clean," he said after a while. "No forgetting. Just… no holding on."

"Some people think that's strength," Gwen replied.

He didn't answer.

The tea in front of him had gone cold. He hadn't taken a single sip.

Outside, the fog pressed close to the glass, softening the edges of the street.

"Perhaps it's better this way," he said at last.

Gwen didn't agree.

Didn't disagree.

She only looked at him for a long, still moment, then said quietly: "Sometimes small conversations are the ones that stay."

Rituals of Abandonment

He used to sweep every morning.

Even when no one came. Even when the wind brought in the same dried leaves, the same fine grit from the stone path outside. It had been habit. A small rite of care, not for the building, but for what it had come to hold.

Now the broom leans against the wall, untouched for days.

A cobweb clings to the baseboard near the south window. One pew is slightly askew. The votive box sits lopsided after someone—maybe him—knocked into it and didn't fix it.

He notices each thing.

Does nothing.

It's not neglect. Not anger. Just an unraveling of attentiveness.

The kind of letting go that doesn't announce itself. That doesn't even feel like a choice. It arrives slowly, like dusk. You don't see it until it's already taken the room.

He doesn't stop entering the chapel.

He simply stops straightening it.

Stops picking up the paper bits near the altar wall. Stops resetting the kneelers. Stops lighting the candle in the corner that once burned every morning before anyone else stirred.

And yet, he's still there.

He sits sometimes, not to think, but because he doesn't know where else to be.

Hands open. Nothing in them.

The silence doesn't press now. It just hovers. Low. Familiar.

Like something abandoned that learned to stay behind anyway.

Her Absence Where It Shouldn't Be

He isn't searching.

But some part of him still checks.

The cabinet where she once placed her sketchbook—empty.

The ledge beneath the stair where her scarf had rested that rainy afternoon—only dust now.

The hook by the back door, where she'd hung her coat once, forgetting it—bare.

He opens these spaces gently. As if anything left behind might still breathe.

But there's nothing. Not even the faintest trace of her perfume. Just a cold neutrality. As if the air had been aired out too thoroughly, as if someone had swept away more than just debris.

She left on purpose, that much he knows.

But it's the completeness of it that undoes him.

Not just her absence.

But the absence of her absence.

No unfinished note. No half-folded page. No echo.

Only a cleanliness that feels… deliberate.

He steps back.

Closes the door slowly.

He doesn't know what he expected—a strand of hair caught on a drawer edge? A smudge on the window? Something.

But there is nothing.

And it is somehow worse than grief.

Because grief suggests something known, something once claimed. This feels more like being erased from a story he thought he had a line in.

He stands there a moment longer, surrounded by everything in place—except the thing that mattered.

Then he turns, the quiet sharp in his chest, and lets the space be what it now is.

Unclaimed. And unclaimable.

Resignation as a Shape

The mist returns with the tide.

Julian walks the cliff path at dusk, the same one he's taken since before she arrived. Same rhythm. Same steps. But something in the air feels heavier now, like the weather knows.

He doesn't carry tools tonight. No pack. No intention. Just his coat, buttoned halfway, and hands in his pockets—where they've stayed too often lately.

The sea below moves without hurry, its surface shifting like thought: slow, reflective, refusing clarity.

He stops where the path bends inland—the place where she once paused to look out.

He doesn't look for her. Not really.

But his eyes scan the haze the way they used to scan the chapel light when he worked late—watching not for movement, but for the feeling of it. That subtle sense that someone else is near. That quiet, electric awareness.

Tonight, there's none of it. Just the wind pushing gently at his collar. Just the sound of gulls farther down the coast.

He closes his eyes.

Her absence is not loud. Not jagged.

It has shape now. It has form. It wraps around his ribs like something tailored—a coat he hadn't noticed he was wearing until it became the only thing keeping him warm.

He doesn't fight it. He doesn't shake it off.

He simply lets it settle.

Then he opens his eyes, steps forward, and continues down the path—not toward anything, not away from anything—just forward.

Because that, for now, is all there is.

A Door Not Closed, Just Unused

Later that night, he walks the long way home.

Past the weathered posts along the bluff. Past the path where the sea disappears behind hedgerows. Past the bakery window, now dark except for the flicker of a motion light catching nothing.

He doesn't know why he turns toward the chapel.

It isn't habit. It isn't hope.

Only some quiet instinct, the kind that moves below words—the same one that told him to leave the door unlocked that morning, though no one had come.

The chapel sits in stillness. No light inside. No sign of her return. But the steps are dry. The leaves swept aside. Not by wind. By someone's hand.

He slows. Pauses.

For a moment, he imagines what it would feel like to open the door again. To step inside. To find something changed— not restored, not repaired, just… altered by her passing through.

But he doesn't cross the threshold.

He doesn't even reach for the handle.

Instead, he looks—really looks—at the door. At the grain of wood worn smooth. At the hinge slightly crooked from years of weather. At the frame that never quite closed cleanly, always a sliver of light left visible from within.

Tonight, the door is shut.

Still unlocked.

He knows because he had not turned the key. He had not wanted to.

He doesn't test it.

Doesn't enter. Doesn't knock.

Just stands there—barely breathing—with the faint sound of waves in the distance and the ache of something unfinished rising again in his chest.

Then, slowly, he turns back toward the road, his shadow folding quietly behind him.

And the chapel remains—closed, yes. But not closed off.

Just… waiting.

Unspoken Recognition

Somewhere, in a room half-lit by the dimming day, Julian stood by the window.

He wasn't expecting anything. Not a knock. Not a letter. But his hand hovered near the sill as if something might arrive all the same.

The chapel had held its silence longer than usual. The sketchbook hadn't moved. The pinecone was gone.

He didn't ask aloud what that meant. Didn't form the words, even inside himself.

But somewhere below thought, beneath the ribs—where knowing settles without explanation—something shifted.

Not sharp. Not sudden. Just a slow, hollowing ache in the gut. The kind that comes when absence is no longer temporary. When something still lives in the air but no longer in reach.

He breathed once, shallow. Then turned from the window. And didn't reach for the light.

Chapter 19

Rituals of Letting Go

The day began without edges. The light outside had arrived softly, like it didn't want to intrude—diffused through a thin veil of mist that clung low to the chapel's roofline and the ridge behind it. Julian stood in the doorway with a cloth in one hand, not to clean, not to fix—just to hold something, because holding something helped delay whatever came next.

It was the kind of morning that didn't announce itself. No sharp sun. No wind. Just the quiet recognition of continuity. A day that looked like yesterday, but wasn't. A day that asked for nothing and still took something from you.

Inside, the chapel smelled faintly of lemon oil and wood dust—residues of care left behind in ordinary gestures. A bench angled slightly in the nave. The broom still resting beside the side wall. Her absence had grown quieter with each day, like it was learning how to belong here too.

Julian crossed the room in measured steps, heel to toe, as though making noise would rupture something sacred. His boots didn't echo. The boards held him as they always had, but he noticed now how the sound of his own movement no longer shared the space with another.

He reached the far window and opened it just a fraction. The sea was barely visible, swallowed in the haze. He could hear it, though—muffled, like it had been softened by memory. It reminded him of the way she used to breathe beside him in the few times they sat near without speaking. How presence alone had once felt like an answer.

He looked at the windowsill, now clear. The pinecone was gone, and he hadn't asked. He had only seen its absence one morning and understood it as a decision.

Some things don't require ceremony to become sacred. Some departures don't knock before they go.

He turned back toward the center of the room, where dust swirled faintly in a shaft of light.

There were no grand resolutions left to make. No long speeches waiting to be written. Only rituals. Small, physical, and ordinary—acts of care with no one to witness them. The kind of movements that let the heart unstick itself, slowly. Quietly.

Julian inhaled, let the breath rest a moment at the top of his chest, then exhaled. One more day. One more set of tasks. Not to finish, not to forget—but to offer the space back to stillness.

And to mean it this time.

Final Details

The rag in Julian's hand had grown soft from use—worn at the corners, the fibers thinned from oil and repetition. He moved it slowly across the chapel floorboards, one plank at a time, following the grain as if retracing something that had already passed. The scent of linseed rose faintly as he worked, mixing with dust and cedar and the distant salt of the sea.

He didn't rush. He rarely did. But there was a different weight in the air now, a hush that lingered not from reverence but from quiet redefinition. The space hadn't lost her. It had simply learned to live without her in it.

In the corner near the entryway, one windowpane bore a crack he hadn't noticed until this morning. It hadn't shattered—just a slow, fanned fracture near the edge, like a splintering thought. He removed the frame carefully and replaced the glass with a smooth new cut he'd had stored for years. It fit without resistance. Clean. Exact.

He stepped back and looked around. The light had shifted slightly across the walls, revealing dust in corners and a pencil line on the stone where someone once measured for a shelf that had never been built.

He crouched by the altar rail, reaching behind the wooden ledge to retrieve a small cloth he thought he'd left tucked there last week. His fingers touched something else—a thin object, smooth and familiar. He drew it out slowly.

A pencil.

The same soft graphite stub she used. One end dulled by use, the other still bearing a faint indentation where she'd rested it between her fingers.

He didn't smile, but something inside him softened.

He turned toward the sill near the back of the chapel—the one that caught the evening sun when it dared to break through. The place where the pinecone had once rested. Where she had lingered in thought.

He set the pencil down gently beside the shallow ashtray he

kept there, now cold.

Not as a relic.

As a gesture.

Not of possession, not of grief. But of presence still acknowledged, even in distance.

A final detail.

Not to finish something. Just to say—It was here. She was here.

And that mattered.

The Compass

Julian hadn't opened the box in years.

It sat beneath the low shelf in his father's old study, behind a stack of warped sketchbooks and a pair of rusted hinges he had always meant to repair. The latch clicked open stiffly, as if the metal itself resisted remembering. Inside, the contents were few—a folded linen handkerchief, a pocketknife dulled from misuse, and the compass.

It rested in a bed of torn velvet lining, brass dulled and spotted with age. He lifted it slowly. The glass face was slightly scratched, the needle sluggish at first but true once it found its direction. North settled into place with a subtle weight, as if it, too, remembered where it belonged.

He turned it in his palm, fingers tracing the worn edge of the casing. The initials on the back—M.V.—had faded with time, but they were still faintly legible, like the memory of a voice you don't hear anymore but can't forget.

Julian didn't carry the compass when he walked. He had never needed it to find his way around Wintermere. But holding it now, he understood something new: direction was not always about movement. Sometimes it was about stillness. About knowing what not to chase.

He brought it back to the chapel and set it on the worktable, beside a strip of sandpaper and the engraving tool he hadn't used in months. He sat for a long while, the compass open beside him, its needle quiet.

Then, on the inner lid, just beneath the hinge, he carved the words with deliberate care:

Not all silence is absence.

The letters were small. Barely visible unless you looked for them. But they were there. A message left for no one—and perhaps for someone. A phrase he might have said aloud, if he'd ever found the courage to turn silence into speech.

He polished the brass gently, then closed the lid with a soft snap. It echoed in the room longer than it should have.

The bench stood near the altar area now, solid and complete. The grain still caught the light in places, and the seat bore the natural curve of a shape made to hold weight without bending. He walked over, compass in hand, and placed it on the center of the bench, angled so its face looked outward toward the sea.

He stepped back.

There was no ceremony. No breath held. No blessing uttered under his breath.

Just a small object, left in plain view.

A compass from the past. A direction he wouldn't follow. And a truth he hoped might reach her, in time or not at all.

The chapel felt different now—not fuller, not empty.

Just honest. Just still.

He found the envelope by chance, though it had likely been there all along.

Tucked between sheets of unused parchment, its flap curled slightly at the edge. Off-white. Unlined. The kind sold in bulk and forgotten in drawers. He held it for a while before doing anything with it—not out of indecision, but because something about the blankness deserved a pause.

There was no card to insert. No folded letter. No message prepared.

Still, he sat at the desk. Picked up a pen. Wrote her name.

Sera

Nothing else.

Not a return address. Not a date.

The ink bled faintly into the paper, soft at the edges like it knew what not to say. He stared at it—not the name itself, but the space around it. The silence that followed. The unspoken that would stay unspoken.

He didn't fill it with words.

He didn't even pretend to.

Instead, he slid the envelope closed with a slow, deliberate motion. No letter inside. No weight beyond the paper itself. And yet, as he pressed the seal down, it felt heavier than it should have. Like it carried what couldn't be written.

Julian stood, walked across the chapel floor with the envelope in his hand. The room was quiet in the way late afternoons sometimes are—shadows stretching longer than seemed natural, the air holding stillness without asking permission.

He placed the envelope gently on the ledge where the altar

had once been, the same place where she had once left her sketch.

It didn't need to be found.

It didn't need to be read.

It only needed to exist—somewhere between offering and absence, between closure and the shape of something that might never fully resolve.

He stepped back.

Didn't look at it again.

Some things, he understood now, were meant to remain sealed—not because they lacked meaning, but because their meaning lived in the act of letting them rest.

He returned to his tools. Ran a cloth slowly across the bench.

And let the silence answer for him.

The Bench

The bench stood finished.

Simple lines. Solid joinery. No ornament.

It had taken longer than it should have—not because the craft was difficult, but because he'd refused to rush. Each joint had been fitted, sanded, oiled by hand. Not out of pride, but because there was no other way to do it right. No shortcuts for something that might carry the weight of someone's pause. Someone's waiting.

He ran his hand across the grain one last time. The wood was warm beneath his palm, even in the early light. Quiet, like it understood what it meant to remain.

Julian crouched at the base. Reached into the small pouch he kept near his tools. Pulled out the fine-point blade.

Near the underside of the right support, just above the

stretch of shadow that would fall every afternoon, he carved three initials.

Not large. Not visible unless you knew where to look.

Not hers. Not his.

Just the shared syllables that sat quietly between them.

J. M. V.

They meant nothing to anyone else. And everything to him.

Julian Mark Vero.

When he finished, he ran his thumb lightly across the carved space. Not to smooth it—just to feel that it was there. The letters were shallow. They would fade with time. Be worn by weather. Disappear into the grain. But for now, they remained. Honest. Hidden.

He stood slowly. Stepped back.

The bench didn't call attention to itself.

It didn't gesture toward sentiment.

It simply *was*—placed with intention, aligned toward the sea-facing window. A resting point. A shelter for silence.

Julian didn't sit.

He let the light fall across the bench, across the initials beneath, across the floorboards he had oiled the day before. Let the stillness return.

There was no ceremony.

Only placement.

Only care.

The Letter Never Sent

He had written it weeks ago. Or maybe only days. Time had become harder to measure lately.

The paper was ordinary—torn from the back of a chapel ledger. The ink, a little uneven where his pen had started to dry.

There was only one line.

Not an apology. Not a question. Just a truth he hadn't known how to say while she was still within reach.

You were never a project.

He folded it once. Then again. No envelope. No salutation. No name.

Some truths didn't need addressing.

That morning, before the light changed, Julian stepped to where the altar had once stood. Found the loose stone in the wall—a place where old notes and candle stubs had once been tucked during Lent or Advent, small signs of devotion left by hands that wanted something but didn't know what.

He slid the paper inside.

Not hidden. But held.

Pressed the stone back into place. Felt the shift of it settle.

And then he stepped away.

He didn't say the words aloud. Didn't linger.

Some letters weren't meant to be sent.

Only placed—so they might outlast the silence.

Chapter 20

The Presentation

The light came earlier than expected, slanting in beneath the chapel's newly cleared rose window, catching specks of dust that hung like ash from an unseen fire. Sera stood just inside the doorway, coat still on, gloves in hand, as though she might leave again. The space ahead of her—quiet, empty for now—was no longer just a project. It was a kept promise. One she hadn't known she was making when she first walked into it.

She stepped forward slowly, her boots brushing against the polished stone, each sound soft, respectful, as if the building were not quite ready to speak. There was something different in the air—less chill, more breath. As if the walls had exhaled after holding it in for too long.

The new pews had been installed without ceremony. The planks were sourced locally—Ruth had helped with that—and left mostly untreated, save for a seal that brought out the natural grain. No gloss, no finish. Just wood that still felt like trees. Sera brushed her fingers along the top of one, grounding herself. She hadn't touched them since the final installation.

She reached the front and turned slowly, taking it all in. The nave had always been narrow, but now, with the back wall cleared and the scaffolding gone, the space breathed wider. Warmer. The soft, natural curvature of the archways drew the eye upward without commanding it, like a hand raised not to demand attention, but to bless it.

And then she saw it.

On the wall just behind where the altar once stood—a panel that hadn't been there before. It was simple. Unpainted. A vertical slab of oak, set into the stone with four visible pegs, each one hand-carved. She moved closer. There, etched faintly in the center, were words:

For what you carried in silence.

The letters weren't signed. No name followed them. But the script, precise yet humble, curved in the way she had seen once before—in a margin, in a sketchbook, in a quiet stroke of graphite left without an ask. She reached out but did not touch it.

Julian had come back. Or perhaps he had never left.

She sat in the first pew, slowly, almost involuntarily. The silence around her wasn't empty. It had grown thick with presence, with echoes that weren't echoes at all but the impression of something never spoken aloud. She wasn't sure how long she sat there. She only knew that soon, others would arrive.

Today wasn't about victory. Not even about closure.

It was about offering.

And whatever remained between them—named or unnamed—had shaped this space, and would now be seen by others.

Not explained. Not defended. Simply seen.

She stood again, gathering herself with a small breath, and

walked toward the rear. As she reached the open doors, she caught her reflection in the side window—taller than she remembered, not because she had grown, but because she had *let go* of what kept her small.

Behind her, the morning light deepened. Ahead, the town waited.

The Room of Faces

They entered as they always did in Wintermere—without fanfare, without hurry. Some came out of obligation, others out of curiosity. A few came with folded arms and narrowed eyes, prepared not to be moved. But most came with that particular Wintermere quiet, the kind that carried with it the weight of generations who had lived beside these stone walls long before the word "revitalization" had become a public matter.

Ruth arrived first, walking without her cane, though slower than usual. She paused at the threshold, eyes sweeping the interior like someone entering a room half-remembered from a childhood dream. Her coat was the color of cranberry bark and she wore a brooch that caught the glass light and fractured it into subtle greens and golds. She offered Sera a glance—just a glance, but it held the calm of someone who knew what had been done here was worth the tension it caused.

Others followed in pairs, in quiet clusters: a fisherman and his wife, still in boots; an older couple who hadn't attended a town meeting in years; Gwen from *Mariner's Rest*, her hair tied back with a ribbon the color of weathered rope. Even Jane arrived, surprisingly, her eyes scanning the room like it might disappear if she looked too fast.

They filled the pews without being told where to sit. It wasn't a performance, and they didn't expect one.

Sera stood near the wall to the side, her notes folded once, then again, tucked into her coat pocket more as an anchor than a reference. She wouldn't read them. She already knew.

As the last few people filed in, she noticed a space toward the back—an empty seat at the far end of the final row. It should have been unremarkable. And yet it drew her attention.

Not the seat itself, but the sense of it.

She looked again. A man was sitting there. At least—she thought he was. Head bowed, posture still. The light didn't quite reach his features. A coat, perhaps brown or grey, hung loosely from his shoulders. His hands were folded, unmoving.

She blinked.

Empty.

No—occupied again.

A shifting of light, or a trick of the angle. Or something deeper. She didn't look a third time.

Instead, she turned her eyes forward as Father Anselm rose from one side and gave the opening word. It wasn't a sermon. Just a welcome, unadorned and brief, his voice gravel-warmed and spare.

"We gather not to dedicate what's been rebuilt," he said. "Only to be present for what has returned."

No one clapped. No one needed to.

In the hush that followed, the sounds of the chapel returned—a creaking beam, a breath, a cough suppressed. The stained glass threw soft lines of blue and amber across the floor like fractured water. Light moved slowly through the room of faces, illuminating one cheek, then another, then gone.

Sera remained still, her back against the stone, not hiding—just waiting. When her time came to speak, she would not be introduced.

She would simply step forward and begin.

Her Proposal

She stepped forward without prompting, the quiet yielding just enough space for movement.

There was no podium, no dais—just the natural front of the chapel, where the altar once stood and where now only light remained. She stood between it and the first row, her figure partially lit by the colored spill of the window behind her. No amplification. No slideshow. Just her voice, and the memory of silence she had come to respect more than any plan she'd once drafted.

Sera unfolded her hands. Not her notes—just her hands. One rested loosely in the other as she paused, not dramatically, but in deference to the space. To the people. To whatever this had become.

"When we began," she said, quietly, "we measured this building by what it lacked."

The room stayed still. No shifting, no murmurs. Just the breath of listening.

"We saw water damage. Sagging beams. Faded paint. No electricity. No heat. And we planned, as planners do, to replace, to modernize, to revise."

A faint sound—perhaps a foot brushing stone—rose from the back. She didn't turn toward it.

"But then something else happened," she continued, her voice steady, though her heart tapped once hard against her ribs. "We stood here long enough to feel what had *stayed*. The air still held the smell of wax and cedar. The walls carried fingerprints, layered over time. Even the cracks had direction."

A few faces softened. Ruth's mouth tilted slightly at one corner, not quite a smile, but something close.

"This building," Sera said, "doesn't ask for relevance. It asks for remembrance."

She let that rest.

"And remembrance," she went on, "is not nostalgia. It's not decoration. It's not sentiment made profitable. It's the act of giving dignity to what made us—even when it no longer serves us in obvious ways."

She reached into her coat pocket—not for her paper, but for a small object she hadn't meant to bring until this morning. A piece of sea glass, smooth and blue. She held it without lifting it.

"In that light," she said, quieter now, "we chose not to modernize. Not to over-polish. Not to replace."

The chapel held its breath.

"We restored the structure where it could hold. We left it bare where it could not. We invited the old air to stay. We made room for what once mattered—to matter again."

She looked toward the third row, where a child now sat on her mother's lap, fingering the end of a scarf. Then toward the back again—without focusing, without fixing. The seat was still empty.

Or not.

"Some places deserve to be remembered," she said, each word falling soft and shaped, "not revised."

Then nothing.

No rhetorical close. No appeal.

She stepped back, the sea glass tucked into her palm.

There was no applause.

Only stillness.

Which, in this place, meant something had been understood.

The Unnamed Presence

The stillness held. Not frozen, but reverent. The kind that lives in the small spaces between perception and memory — not quite silence, not quite sound.

Sera did not return to the wall this time. She remained near the edge of the front pew, standing—not to assert, not to lead, but simply to stay. Her presence there was not command but witness.

Ruth shifted slightly in her seat and glanced around. She wasn't looking for anything in particular, but her eyes came to rest on Sera, as if hearing something still echoing in the air. Something familiar, though not previously hers.

Sera hadn't meant to speak like him. But the phrasing, the hesitations, the way her voice dropped just before the final word in a sentence—it was not her usual cadence. It had softened. It had curved in places where once it cut. There were pauses that felt less strategic, more sacred. She was, without knowing, echoing the silence of another voice.

Gwen caught it too. Not consciously, not with analysis, but in the way a body recognizes temperature before the mind gives it name. She leaned forward slightly, the way one does when listening for a note that only appears on the second hearing.

Someone near the back row nodded—barely perceptible, the

gesture of someone agreeing with something deeper than words. Their face remained still, but the motion was instinctive. Not affirmation of a proposal, but of a presence.

Julian, if he was there, did not move. Did not shift. But the room was not empty of him.

The way the light filtered now—more golden than blue—gave the sense that something had arrived, or perhaps had been there all along. That feeling, when someone stands behind you quietly, not touching, not breathing loud, but *felt* nonetheless.

Sera didn't turn around. She didn't need to.

His name wasn't spoken. Not in words. But he was in the timbre of the room now—in the woodgrain she had chosen not to sand, in the flicker of blue in the window glass, in the way she had described time not as a line, but as a shelter.

His absence was not a void.

It was a thread. Present only when the tapestry was viewed as a whole.

She rested her hands in front of her again, the sea glass still in her palm, growing warm. She could not say why, but the act of holding it grounded her—not to memory, but to clarity. She had spoken what needed to be said. To the town. And, in some indirect way, to him.

It would be enough.

Or it would not.

But it was real.

The Vote

There was no formal call to action, no procedural pivot. Yet the moment turned gently toward decision, as if carried there by the weight of silence itself.

A rustle of motion came from the center row—Harold Mason, the longtime councilman who rarely spoke unless prompted, cleared his throat and stood. He didn't raise his voice. Didn't make a speech.

"I move to accept the proposal as presented," he said. "Without revisions."

No second was asked for. But Ruth gave it anyway, her voice calm and sure.

"All in favor?"

It was Father Anselm who asked, not as chair, not by title, but as one accustomed to reading a room's reverence.

Hands rose—not all at once, but in waves. A nod from Gwen. A firm lift from the fisherman near the aisle. Even Jane, eyes narrowed, voted with a quiet conviction that surprised even herself.

One or two abstained. None opposed.

There was no cheer. No rise of applause. Only a slow exhale, like something long held had finally been released.

A woman in the second row—Miriam, who once protested the budget—wiped a tear that had crept down without her noticing. She didn't dab it with embarrassment. She let it fall, then folded her hands.

A man near the back clapped. Just once.

Not for performance. Not for ceremony. Just once, and then he stopped.

Sera bowed her head slightly. Not in thanks. Not in triumph. Not even in relief.

It was something older than all those things. Something

quieter.

Recognition.

That this place had spoken. That she had heard it. That the town, in its own way, had listened too.

She closed her eyes briefly, not to shut the moment out, but to let it settle within. Then opened them again, slowly, as light broke across the far wall—rose-tinted, like the inside of a shell.

Whatever this had been—a proposal, a plea, a benediction— it was now shared.

Not possessed.

And in Wintermere, that meant it belonged.

Stillness, Again

The room emptied the way it had filled—without instruction, without rush.

A few paused near the back to murmur a word to Ruth or nod in Father Anselm's direction. Gwen lingered near one of the windows, her fingers trailing the edge of a frame before slipping into her coat. Jane left without comment, her exit as soft as her entrance.

Soon, there were only footfalls. Then the quiet that returns when a place is given back to itself.

Sera remained near the front, not out of obligation, but because she couldn't yet move. Her legs were not heavy, exactly. They simply refused to treat the moment as done.

She stepped forward, slowly, until she stood once more before the panel.

For what you carried in silence.

The light had shifted across the carved words now, making

some letters appear deeper, others fading into grain. It felt less like a message than a memory caught in wood. Something left, not for display, but for understanding.

She did not touch it.

Instead, she walked to the center aisle, pausing halfway back, then veered toward the pew where she had seen—or imagined—him.

The seat was empty.

But the air still held a shape. The way a room feels after someone stands and leaves their warmth behind. She sat, slowly, folding into the space he might have filled, as if proximity could conjure meaning, or comfort, or simply *witness*.

In her palm, the sea glass remained. Smooth now, warm. She placed it on the pew beside her, just for a moment. As if letting it breathe.

Then she looked up.

The stained glass cast a quiet geometry of color across the floor—amber, blue, a hint of green. No single ray fell on her, and that felt right. This was not her light. It was shared.

She drew in a breath—not a sigh, but something deeper. A breath that did not need to be answered.

Then she stood.

No ceremony. No gesture.

Just standing. Fully.

At the rear of the chapel, she turned back for one last glance.

Not to assess. Not to admire.

Just to *see*.

The room held no applause. No echo. But it held something else now. Something more complete.

Stillness, yes.
But no longer emptiness.

Chapter 21

The Door He Left Open

She arrived before the frost had finished settling. The mist along the chapel's roofline held its shape longer in the cold—curling like breath held too long against stone. Sera stepped into the courtyard without checking the time, her boots leaving soft impressions in the white-tinged gravel, which melted slightly beneath the pressure of each step.

The door was already unlocked. She didn't question it.

Inside, the air was unmoving. Not cold exactly, but not yet warmed by day. The kind of stillness that felt less like emptiness and more like waiting. She did not speak. She only stood there, just past the threshold, her hand still on the door, as if unsure whether to release it or hold it open longer—for someone, or something, unnamed.

Eventually, she stepped fully inside and let the door ease closed behind her with the soft pull of memory.

The chapel hadn't changed. But it had settled. There was a sense that the building had taken a long breath since the gathering two days prior—and now exhaled in her presence. It did not feel expectant. It felt known.

She made her way forward slowly, fingertips brushing the edge of a bench, the grain worn to a gentle smoothness by more than just time. Dust moved in the shaft of morning light, each fleck suspended like ash. She reached the front without thinking and paused in the space between altar rail and pew.

A candle had been left—short, unlit, near the window ledge.

She struck a match from the box tucked into her coat's inside pocket. Lit it with a small gesture. Watched the flame hesitate, then claim the wick without ceremony. It wavered once. Then steadied.

She set the match aside and sat—not in the front pew, not at the side, but in the third row, slightly off center. The place she once imagined someone else might sit.

The chapel was not hers.

Not anymore.

But it was not foreign, either.

She closed her eyes—not to pray, not to rest—but to hold stillness without bracing against it.

Outside, the frost began to lift from the rooftops. And inside, the door remained closed.

For now.

Discovered, Not Offered

The chapel held its silence like breath held just past the point of speaking.

Sera remained seated for some time in the third pew, her eyes open but unfixed, the candlelight flickering across the corners of her coat. Outside, frost receded slowly from the stone path, but in here the light was steady, warm in tone, if not in temperature.

Eventually, she rose—not abruptly, but with the same kind

of quiet certainty that had brought her here. Her steps made no sound this time. She moved not forward but to the side, toward the narrow passage near the vestry wall. The door to the hidden room was still ajar, just enough to suggest it had been visited recently, or not fully left.

She entered.

The air inside was cooler, still edged with the scent of wood and something faintly mineral, like damp stone or old paper. The desk was untouched. The chair—simple, sturdy—still angled toward the icon in the corner. Nothing had changed. And yet—

On the desk, near the far edge, lay something she hadn't seen before.

Not prominently placed, not offered. Almost overlooked.

She stepped closer.

A compass.

It rested without ceremony on the woodgrain, its casing dulled, the brass worn smooth at the edges. No note. No sign of its placement.

She reached for it—not urgently, not cautiously. Her fingers closed around the metal with an ease that surprised her.

It was light. But it carried weight.

She turned it once in her palm, and again. The needle wavered gently, then found its line. North, or some version of it. But it wasn't direction she felt—it was memory. Something older than maps. Something quieter than guidance.

She didn't smile. Her face stayed still. But something inside her shifted—not like a door opening, but like air entering a sealed room.

She slipped the compass into the inner pocket of her coat.

Not to hide it, but to carry it.

Then she stepped back into the chapel's main hall, her feet moving without noise. The candle still burned. The pews remained empty.

But not for long.

The light behind her changed.

And she didn't need to turn to know he had entered.

The Encounter

She heard him before she saw him.

Not footsteps, not breath—but the faint shift in the room's stillness, as if something living had passed through a line of sunlight and changed the shape of air. The kind of presence you feel in your spine before your mind names it.

She didn't turn.

She remained seated in the pew, eyes forward, hands resting loosely on her lap. The compass was still tucked inside her coat, though its shape pressed lightly through the fabric—a small weight near her ribs, steadying.

He entered without pause, without noise. Julian's movements were always composed, but today there was something different in the way he crossed the chapel threshold. Not guarded. Not cautious. But bare. He carried nothing. No crate. No tools. No coat.

Just himself.

She rose slowly, turning to face him—her expression unreadable but not closed. Her eyes met his, and neither looked away.

It had been weeks. Maybe longer. The space between them

had stretched, retracted, bent with choice and ache and silence. But now they stood on level ground—not as architect and builder, not as project lead and contractor—but as two people shaped by the same place, the same quiet, the same unsent messages.

Julian's gaze dropped briefly, then returned.

She reached into her coat and withdrew the compass.

Held it in her open palm. Not as a question. Not as an accusation.

Just as truth.

His eyes rested on it. No surprise. No explanation. Only recognition—the kind that comes when something shared finally has shape.

Still, he did not reach for it.

And she did not offer it.

A long moment passed.

Then, wordlessly, she stepped aside and moved toward the far bench — the one that had always leaned slightly to the left, askew no matter how often it was nudged back into line.

Julian followed.

The Shared Movement

The bench was just slightly off—not enough to be noticed by most, but enough that she and Julian both paused before it. One leg had caught on the edge of a floor stone, making the line skew gently toward the aisle.

They didn't speak.

Sera crouched at one end, placing her fingers beneath the worn edge of the seat. Julian mirrored her at the other. In sync, they lifted—just enough to shift—and eased it back into place. The sound of wood brushing stone filled the space between them. A friction softened by long use.

It wasn't the act itself that mattered.

It was the fact that neither had to gesture. Neither had to ask.

They simply saw—and moved.

Once the bench was righted, she didn't rise immediately. Instead, she remained there, one knee still bent, hand resting on the seat. Then, reaching into her coat once more, she pulled out an envelope—thick, hand-folded, its edges slightly softened from having been carried for days.

She stood and walked toward him.

Held it out.

Two hands. No flourish.

He accepted it with the same stillness with which she'd offered it. No glance inside. No hesitation. He held it gently, as if its contents were known even without being read. And perhaps they were.

There was no question of opening it now. That wasn't its purpose.

She moved toward the newly adjusted bench and sat down. Not at the far edge, and not at the center. Somewhere in between.

He followed a moment later, lowering himself beside her— not too close, but near enough that the heat of his arm touched the air beside her sleeve. Their shoulders did not touch. But their nearness shifted something in the space.

Outside, the wind stirred faintly against the chapel's exterior, the low groan of tree limbs audible through the old stone.

Inside, the silence deepened.

But it held no tension.

No waiting.

Only presence.

The Settlement

The envelope lay on the bench between them, untouched.

Neither looked at it.

They sat in stillness for a long while—not in paralysis, not in expectation, but in something else. A kind of peace that did not need to name itself. The chapel had taken on a different tone in their presence—not brighter, not warmer, but clearer, as though its walls recognized them now not as occupants but as contributors to its becoming.

The silence was not the silence they had once shared—the taut, aching kind that came from words withheld or meanings sidestepped. This one held no pull, no edge. It was round, spacious, breathable.

Sera drew in a slow breath and released it through her nose. Her gaze remained forward, not on the windows or the empty front of the room, but on the floor where the light cut across the stone—gold against gray. Julian's hands rested on his knees, steady, calloused. The same hands that had once carried wood across the threshold, lifted beams into place, righted the chapel's bones when no one else believed they were worth saving.

Now they carried nothing.

And still, they held everything.

At one point, his shoulder shifted slightly toward her—not to close the space, but to recognize it.

She did not move away.

They remained like that, still and aligned, until the sun lifted higher through the windows and the shape of the light changed on the floor. Neither marked the time. There was no schedule. No outcome. Just the fact of being here, together, after everything that had passed through them—silence, doubt, offering, loss.

The chapel no longer belonged to her design, her proposal, or his solitude. It belonged to something they had shaped together. Something that would hold even after they stood up and walked out.

Sera turned, not fully, just enough to see the edge of his profile.

"Thank you," she said, barely above breath. Not for the compass. Not for the bench. For everything that had never needed to be said but had, somehow, still been heard.

Julian nodded once. His eyes didn't leave the light.

And that was enough.

Chapter 22

The Quiet One

The light arrived before they moved. It crept in quiet bands across the stone floor, warming the edges of the bench where they still sat—not speaking, not drifting, simply *there*. The day had risen without announcement, and neither of them had checked a watch or noted the hour. Time had settled into something slower, shaped less by clocks than by presence.

Julian shifted once, adjusting the envelope that still rested between them. He didn't open it. She didn't press. It was enough that it existed between them—seen, unclaimed, understood.

The compass remained inside her coat. She could feel its weight now not as question or origin, but as part of her. A kept thing. A known thing.

There was no need to start again. No need to revisit what had passed, or to name what had grown in the quiet spaces between them. They had already crossed the distance. What remained was *not proof*, not promise—but something softer. A belonging that required no definition.

Outside, the wind moved low along the chapel walls, brushing against stone and frame with the gentleness of breath.

Inside, the air shifted only when one of them exhaled—and even that felt like a shared act.

They didn't plan to rise at the same time. But when they did, it felt natural. Wordless. Right.

Sera reached for her coat. Julian stood without needing to be asked. The bench, now straightened, remained behind them—smooth, solid, held in the angle they had chosen together.

And the light kept growing.

The Room Restored

The chapel no longer asked anything of them.

No project remained. No decisions awaited approval. There were no more boards to level, no reports to file, no votes to cast. The room stood not as a question now, but as a kind of response—to care, to patience, to the things we build when we stop trying to possess them.

Julian walked to the rear of the chapel, where a loose hinge on the inner door had caught unevenly for weeks. He didn't need to fix it. And yet he crouched down, pulled a small brass wedge from the inner lining of his coat—something carried for days, maybe longer—and pressed it quietly beneath the edge. The movement took only a moment. But it steadied the frame.

Sera didn't watch him do it. Not directly. She walked the perimeter slowly instead, her fingers grazing the inner stone columns, as if reacquainting herself with their form not as materials, but as memory.

The chapel breathed differently now.

It wasn't the light—though the morning sun had taken on a clearer hue, gold streaking diagonally across the worn stone floor and lifting dust into momentary orbit. It wasn't the silence either, though that too had changed. It was the sense that nothing was being held back anymore.

She reached the eastern wall and paused beneath the window—the one they had once uncovered behind a collapsed beam. Its panes were thin and irregular, imperfect in their lead lines, but luminous. The glass glowed now, soft amber and pale green, casting ribbons of warmth onto the far pews.

Her drawing hung just beside it.

Still unsigned. Still unframed. Mounted with quiet intention—no plaque, no announcement, no name.

Just a gesture made visible.

Julian approached and stood beside her, his eyes taking in the sketch. The lines were faint but deliberate—the bones of the chapel, rendered not as it had been, but as it had become. The window. The bench. A door half open. A figure in the background, barely visible, almost ghosted into the shading.

He didn't ask if it was meant to be him. He didn't need to.

Sera looked at it for a moment longer. Then turned slightly, her gaze falling to the bench behind them. It had held. The two of them had righted it the day before—or was it just earlier that morning? Time no longer held to neat divisions. What mattered was that it remained level, solid, and now somehow central to the room. Not just a place to sit. A place that held their quiet labor, their shared effort, the pauses that had once gone unnamed.

Julian sat down.

No words.

Just the soft creak of wood and the slow settling of weight.

Sera joined him a breath later, her coat now folded over one arm, the lines of her shoulder relaxed in a way they hadn't been in months. She didn't sit precisely beside him, but close—not avoiding touch, not seeking it. Just near enough that their presence acknowledged the other without leaning on it.

The light through the window moved. It now caught the compass shape beneath her coat, tracing a faint gleam beneath the fabric. She let it remain there—not as a secret, not as a symbol, just as something carried forward.

They sat like that for some time.

Letting the room hold them.

The drawing on the wall. The bench beneath. The door propped open just slightly to the world beyond.

There was no declaration to be made. No next step. No final line to draw. Only the quiet knowledge that the chapel was no longer a site of repair—not for the building, and not for them.

It had become a space of **belonging**.

And that was enough.

What They Don't Say

They moved without signal, without cue.

From the bench, they rose together—not with urgency, and not as one, but as if their bodies had memorized the rhythm of the room and followed it without effort. Julian walked first, tracing a familiar arc along the side aisle, while Sera moved through the center, her hand brushing the top of each pew in passing, like quiet acknowledgments. They arrived at the front almost simultaneously.

There was no altar anymore.

Not in the formal sense—the marble slab that once stood at the head of the chapel had been removed long before the project began, left crumbled and unclaimed behind the property's far shed. Nothing had replaced it. And yet the space where it once stood still held its shape—an invisible boundary marked not by stone, but by attention.

They stood there now, not across from one another, but beside each other, facing forward. Not toward faith. Not toward memory. Just toward space.

Sera's hands were bare, her coat slung gently over one forearm. The cold didn't reach her here. Or perhaps she no longer registered it. Julian kept his hands at his sides, fingers loose, relaxed. The silence that settled between them wasn't constructed. It didn't feel ceremonial. It simply *was*.

For a long moment, they stood like that. Breathing. Listening.

There was no wind, but the chapel made sound nonetheless—the faint groan of old wood in the ceiling joists, the creak of distant floorboards settling into themselves, the dry tap of dust shifting across a windowsill. Small sounds. Familiar ones.

His hand moved first.

Not dramatically. Not deliberately.

It drifted, almost as if caught in the draw of light, and grazed the back of her hand—just a brush of warmth against the skin below her knuckle. The contact was feather-light, nearly mistakable. But she didn't pull away.

She didn't move at all.

His fingers hovered there for a second longer, then stilled. They didn't intertwine. They didn't close. They simply *rested*, near enough to feel the heat of one another's palm, the pulse of proximity.

Her breath deepened—not sharp, not shaky, but round. A breath shared, not held. As if her body understood something before her mind had to name it.

Still, they said nothing.

There were words that could be spoken—sentences they had circled around for weeks, maybe months—but none were necessary now. The silence between them was no longer a wall or a wound. It had shape, texture. It *held*.

Julian shifted slightly, his weight moving to his left foot. Sera's shoulder rose and fell in a slow, even rhythm. Their bodies did not lean, but they aligned—a quiet geometry of presence, unspoken and intact.

They didn't look at each other.

They looked forward.

To the light. To the room. To the space that had once asked for transformation and now simply offered itself—unfinished, whole, and gently luminous.

Their hands remained near. Their silence unbroken.

And what they didn't say filled the room with more meaning than speech ever could.

The Gesture

She reached into her coat without looking down.

The movement was slow, almost imperceptible at first—her fingers grazing the inner lining, pausing as if to remember what they were searching for. But the object had been there all along, tucked in the same fold where she'd kept the compass. She hadn't touched it since placing it there. But its shape was known to her now, familiar not in weight but in meaning.

Her hand emerged, closed around the sea glass.

She looked at it for the first time in days—a piece no larger than a coin, worn smooth at the edges, its green translucent and softened by time. Not perfectly round, not sharp, not remarkable to anyone else. But it had carried something forward. A trace of a moment. A presence she hadn't been able to name until now.

Julian noticed, but did not ask.

He had not moved since their hands had brushed. He stood beside her, his gaze lowered slightly, not on her hand but toward the altar's former space—that wide openness that no longer sought designation. Only offering.

Sera stepped forward, just a pace.

No ceremony. No hesitation.

She reached the window ledge to the side—the one they had once cleared together of debris and splinters and years of damp neglect. The light from the eastern glass poured down onto the sill like a quiet stream. Resting there already was the thin gray circle of ash from a long-extinguished candle. Beside it: the compass, gently placed just that morning. Not arranged. Not staged. Just present.

She added the sea glass to them.

Placed it without drama, without centering it. It tilted slightly against the frame of the compass, catching the light at its edge. For a moment it seemed to glow—not with brightness, but with memory. The kind of glow that only happens when something finds its right place.

An altar, accidental and true.

Three objects. Nothing of value. Nothing spoken.

But each held something: orientation, remnants, and witness.

Behind her, Julian stepped forward—not to follow, not to

join, but to meet her at a different distance. His hand hovered just at her back—not touching, not pressing, but near. A proximity that wasn't possessive, wasn't directive. Just *with*.

Sera didn't turn around, but she felt it. That nearness. The way his presence had always announced itself first in silence. It steadied her.

She looked at the items on the sill one more time, then slowly let her arm return to her side.

Their eyes met a moment later—she turned slightly, just enough to meet his gaze.

What passed between them wasn't a question. It wasn't resolution. It was recognition. A shared knowing.

You brought this. I carried that. We left it here.

And now, here it remains.

His gaze softened, but he didn't smile. She didn't either.

Because there are gestures that do not require response.

There are offerings not made to be answered, only understood.

And in that moment, what they had built—with hands and silences, with drawings and benches, with letters not read and names not spoken—had found its expression in the simplest thing: something left behind, together.

What Remains

They stepped through the door he had once left open—not quickly, not hesitantly, but as if time itself had softened its grip on them.

There was no moment of pause on the threshold. No backward glance. Only the sound of gravel shifting beneath their feet and the low rustle of wind making its way through the chapel courtyard, brushing against the edges of things left behind.

They did not speak.

But their closeness no longer needed proof. It moved with them—in the way their steps found a shared cadence, in the way their silences no longer scraped against longing but held space for something deeper. Not certainty. Not conclusion. But presence, unguarded.

The morning had lifted into a pale warmth. Not bright, but clear. The kind of clarity that reveals without demanding. Behind them, St. Avila's stood in stillness. The sea glass, the compass, and the ash remained on the sill, catching the new light without fanfare. The drawing beside the window hung just as she had placed it— not as a statement, but as a trace.

They walked together down the narrow path, past the hedgerow, past the stone curve of the wall where moss grew thickest. The air carried the scent of salt and slow beginnings.

As they neared the lane, Julian's hand reached gently across the space between them. Not grasping. Not asking.

Just a light touch—fingers brushing against hers, then settling, loose and unforced, into the spaces where her fingers waited without meaning to.

She didn't look down. She didn't look at him.

But something passed between them—not a signal, not a word, but warmth. Immediate. Quiet. Known.

It moved through her palm and into her chest like heat rising from the earth after rain. He felt it too—not in his hand, but somewhere in his gut. The unmistakable recognition of something longed for that has stopped hiding.

They walked on like that—joined, but not claimed. Connected, but not contained.

At the lane, their bodies slowed, as if arriving at something unspoken. They turned slightly—not toward each other, but into their own directions. The hands slipped apart without loss. The warmth remained.

There was no vow exchanged. No future planned aloud. But something had settled in the space between them. A closing of one kind. An opening of another.

Sera's breath rose and left her slowly. Julian's gaze drifted toward the chapel once more, then returned to the road ahead. They shared one final glance—brief, unmarred by weight—and then, with nothing said, they moved on.

Not together. Not away from each other. But forward.

In the wake of so much unsaid, something had found its shape. And that shape did not require answers. Only the quiet courage to live within its truth.

What remained was not possession. Not memory.

But the trace of presence. And the knowing that love, when it is real, does not always arrive with clarity—but it stays.

Even as they disappeared into the path's vanishing point, the door remained open.

And behind it, the light held.

Epilogue

After Stillness

The wind moved differently now around St. Avila's. Not stronger, not softer—just settled, as if the chapel no longer braced against time but breathed with it. Morning light didn't rush through the windows the way it once had. It drifted, lingered, found corners and stayed.

The chapel had no posted hours. No plaque bore the names of those who steadied its walls. It remained unlocked more often than not, not out of duty, but because it made sense. People came. Or didn't. But the space was never vacant.

For those who stepped inside with quiet steps—and ears tuned to something beneath silence—there was a sense of memory still moving. Not past. Not lost. But continuous.

Not a story concluded. But one still unfolding—without names, without claims. Just presence, lived and left behind.

The Place Remains

St. Avila's no longer needed introduction. It stood at the end of the path, just beyond the bend, where the hedgerow bowed slightly and the gravel thinned. No signs. No banners. No inscription above the door. It asked nothing of those who approached.

The restoration had never been recorded in any local paper. There was no grant recognition, no gold-embossed name etched into a brick. The records at the historical society made passing mention of "light structural reinforcement completed mid-season," but no mention of who had carried the beams, or who had brushed the dust from the sill beside the window. That part of the story remained unwritten. Or perhaps it had been written in materials more lasting than ink.

Inside, the pews wore their smoothness without apology. The room was not pristine. It didn't gleam. Instead, it exhaled a kind of quiet earned only by places that had been loved without spectacle.

Dust still gathered in the corners. Rain still whispered through the roof beams when the wind pressed in from the east. But nothing had been left untended. A new coat of oil had darkened the doors, making the grain more visible. The floor had settled into its creaks and softened edges. Even the air felt different—not stale or reverent, but *known*.

At the front of the chapel, where the altar once stood, there remained only the light. It pooled along the stone and stretched out across the floorboards in the early hours, as if laying itself down to rest. There were no candles now. No incense. No scripture or sermon. Just space. And presence.

Some came expecting more—more signs of transformation, more explanation, perhaps even a docent to narrate what had been done. They often left quietly. Not disappointed, but hushed in a different way. As if realizing the story here wasn't something told aloud, but something listened for.

The place didn't offer answers. But it remained.

And sometimes, that was the only invitation needed.

The Unknown Ritual

Visitors come. Not in droves. But steadily.

Some arrive with purpose—locals who remember the renovations, or who've heard whispers of what was once a proposal and then, somehow, something more. They come with a reverence that doesn't ask to be named, walking the path in slow steps, pausing at the door not because they're unsure, but because they feel—viscerally—that entry means *something*. Even now.

Others come by chance. A couple on a weekend walk. A photographer following the shape of light through unfamiliar towns. A traveler looking for a place to stretch, who ends up sitting far longer than they meant to. These visitors do not know its name, but they speak of its quiet as if they've returned from somewhere rather than stumbled into it.

They do not speak much inside. Or if they do, it is with hushed voices—words trailing off mid-thought, as though spoken language might fracture whatever is held in the walls. Some sit for only a few moments. Others linger until dusk stretches long across the floor. Some kneel without realizing it. Some close their eyes and simply listen.

There are no services. No sermons. No structure, schedule, or rite.

And yet something happens.

They arrive with stories pressed tight in their chests. Regrets not yet grieved. Decisions yet unmade. Lonelinesses too complicated to name. They do not always know why they've come.

And still, many leave with something shifted—lightened, yes, but not erased. As if a burden had been acknowledged by something larger than themselves. Not taken. Just seen.

Sometimes, a visitor will leave behind an object. A pressed leaf. A folded note, never signed. A scrap of ribbon, a coin, a single page torn from a notebook. These offerings never pile. They never draw attention. And somehow, they always disappear by the next season—cleared away not by staff, for there are none, but perhaps by the place itself. Or by hands that know not to take, only to carry.

Children visit too, now and then. A teacher once brought her class as part of a walking history lesson, unsure whether the stop would hold their attention. But the children grew quiet as they stepped inside. One child whispered, "It feels like someone's listening." The others nodded.

And still, the chapel asks for nothing.

It is not a destination. It is not a museum. It is not a sacred site in the traditional sense. But something sacred has been carried here, and left behind—not as relic, but as rhythm. As breath. As presence without proclamation.

The ritual is not known. But it is felt.

It exists in the act of entering, of pausing, of letting silence answer silence. Of recognizing that in a world flooded with explanation and display, there remains at least one room where nothing is required but *being*.

And for those who leave with less weight than they arrived with, there is no language to describe why.

Only the quiet knowing that something within them had been heard.

Even if no one spoke at all.

They appear without fail.

Not daily. Not always predictably. But often enough that those who come to St. Avila's begin to expect them, even if they don't realize it at first.

A small bunch of wildflowers, left on the front bench. Always in the same spot—just slightly right of center, where the wood dips faintly from years of use. The stems lean gently against the edge of the seat, never upright, never formal. As if placed by a hand that wasn't concerned with presentation, only offering.

They are never arranged. Not clipped to uniform height. Not sorted by color or type. One week, soft yellow primroses and blue flax. Another, white clover and fireweed. Occasionally, something bolder—a stray thistle, or a single blood-red poppy, wilted at the edges but still holding its color like a stubborn truth. The combinations make no aesthetic sense. And yet, no one ever calls them messy.

They're always fresh. Not from a store. Not bouquet-wrapped. But gathered—somehow. Picked, it seems, from the same hedgerow that curves along the path, or from the fields just beyond the lane. Wild. Unnamed. Intact.

What draws the most quiet attention is the string.

Each bundle is tied with a thin piece of faded blue twine. Not ribbon. Not tape. Just a simple loop, knotted once, frayed at the ends. The kind of string one might find in a drawer with old maps or forgotten keys. It never changes color. Always the same blue. Softened by weather, age, or use.

No one has ever seen the flowers being placed.

A few locals have tried. An older man who walks the path

each morning timed his route earlier and earlier, hoping to catch the unknown hand in the act. A young girl once claimed she saw someone from a distance, just a figure in the mist. But when pressed, she admitted she wasn't sure if she'd dreamed it. The air, she said, felt like it does right before it snows. "Quiet in a round way."

Some say it's an old woman from the north lane—one who rarely speaks but once tended a garden behind the post office. Others believe it's a group of children from the schoolhouse who made a pact never to reveal their secret. A man from out of town suggested it might be a tradition passed down by previous caretakers. But there is no record of caretakers. Not officially.

Still, the flowers come.

And over time, their presence has become part of the place. Like the light that filters through the high window at mid-morning. Like the compass still resting in the corner of the sill, dulled but unmoved. Like the faint creak of the door hinge that no one ever seems to fix.

People don't speak of the flowers as tribute. Or decoration. They speak of them the way one might speak of memory. Or breath.

Their presence doesn't seek attention. It grants it.

And though the petals never face the same direction twice, though the stems lean left one week and right the next, the wildflowers always carry a certain weightless knowing. A kind of quiet that doesn't ask for recognition.

Only continuity.

Only love, left without announcement.

Only the kind of care that slips past language, but never goes unnoticed.

Two Figures

Sometimes, at first light. Other times, just before dusk folds the sky into its own hush.

There, near the chapel—but not on the path, and not at the door—a pair of figures can sometimes be seen. Still. Unmoving. Not statues. Not ghosts. Just human enough to be real, and just distant enough to feel almost imagined.

They do not arrive. They are not seen leaving.

They are simply… there.

One stands slightly behind the other, but never too far. Their shapes are unremarkable to the casual eye—no bold gestures, no clothing that sets them apart. But to those who pause long enough to truly look, something unmistakable gathers in the space between them.

A pause that is not absence.

A stillness that is not silence.

As if whatever passes between them has no need of words, because it has already passed through the fire of them.

They do not touch. But their nearness bends the light in subtle ways—gathering where it shouldn't, softening where it might have broken. Sometimes a hand lifts, loosely, not extended and not withheld. Sometimes a shoulder leans just slightly. A gesture half-buried in restraint.

Most visitors don't notice.

Those who come only once often miss them entirely—or see only a blur of form by the edge of the hedgerow. Some say it's just the angle of morning sun, or mist pooling in suggestion. Others call it memory, made visible by the stories that locals still don't tell aloud.

But some do see them.

The ones who return.

The ones who stay longer than they meant to.

The ones who sit without checking the time, and feel a warmth along their spine that has nothing to do with sun.

They do not speak of it. Not immediately.

But they carry something with them when they leave. A gentling of breath. A loosening in the chest. A recognition without name.

To them, the figures are real.

Real the way wind is real—felt, but never held.

Real the way a name lingers, even when it hasn't been spoken in years.

Some say the figures are nothing.

Just the trick of light. Just presence mistaken for meaning.

But others—

The ones who notice the hush before the door creaks open. The ones who bring nothing in and still leave lighter.

The ones who begin to understand that the chapel offers no history, only continuity—

They say the stillness between the figures speaks.

It does not speak of endings.

Or of certainty. Or even of answers.

It speaks of a different kind of bond.

One that does not depend on naming, or claiming, or resolution.

It speaks of something shaped not by possession, but by return.

Of gestures made and remade in silence. Of love that was

never declared, but never denied.

Something here, they say, was loved into being.

And never left.

Some around town don't say their names, but they nod softly when the topic drifts near. They just smile gently when the two are mentioned—as if the truth has always been part of the place itself, folded into its grain like warmth into worn wood.

———————————————

It's nothing. Just part of the place now.

But those who notice say:

Something here was loved into being.

And never left.

About the Author

Cameron Lane writes stories about second chances, transformation, and the unseen forces that shape our lives. Best known for *The Squaring of a Heart*, a quietly powerful novel of healing and relational repair, Cameron's work explores the liminal spaces between love and loss, silence and connection, past and possibility.

Blending heartwarming small-town settings with deeper journeys of spirit and resilience, Cameron's fiction invites readers into emotional landscapes where restoration unfolds one quiet gesture at a time.

When not writing, Cameron enjoys wandering the unfamiliar, collecting traces of heritage, and reflecting on the spaces where light meets shadow.

Book Club Discussion Guide

Introduction for Book Clubs

The Quiet One is a literary novel about presence, silence, and the invisible architecture of love. It invites readers to slow down, to feel rather than analyze, and to witness a romance that forms not through confession but through restoration—of places, of people, and of trust.

This guide offers a set of questions and reflection prompts to deepen your group's conversation. Some are thematic. Others are personal. None require answers—only presence.

Part I: General Discussion Questions

1. Stillness as Language
   - What role does silence play in the relationship between Julian and Sera?
   - Did the absence of direct dialogue deepen or distance your emotional connection to the story?

2. Place as Character
   - How does St. Avila's chapel function as more than a setting?
   - In what ways does the restoration of the chapel mirror the emotional journey of the characters?

3. Gesture Over Declaration
   - The novel avoids grand romantic gestures. What do you think is the most emotionally significant act in the story?
   - How does the novel challenge traditional ideas of romantic storytelling?

4. The Unspoken and the Unfinished

o Why do you think the altar was never replaced?

o How does the idea of something incomplete add to the spiritual resonance of the story?

5. Presence Without Possession

o Discuss how intimacy is built in the novel. How is this different from most modern depictions of love?

Part II: Character-Centered Prompts

6. Julian Vero

o How did your impression of Julian evolve throughout the book?

o In what ways does he reflect or resist the idea of a "quiet strength"?

7. Sera Linden

o How does Sera's journey reflect the theme of reclamation—not just of space, but of self?

o What makes her drawn to Julian, and what holds her back?

8. Supporting Figures

o What roles do characters like Gwen or Father Anselm play in the emotional fabric of the story?

o Were there any minor characters you wished to see more of?

Part III: Reflective & Personal

9. A Room That Listens

o Have you ever encountered a space that felt like St. Avila's—quiet, sacred, and healing?

o What do you think your own version of the chapel might be?

10. Unspoken Connections

o Have you ever shared a bond that wasn't verbal, but deeply felt?

o How do these relationships shape who we become?

11. Love Without Naming

o The novel suggests that some forms of love do not need to be named. Do you agree?

o Can love exist without confession? Without resolution?

Final Question for the Group

"Something here was loved into being. And never left." What do you think that "something" is—for the story? For you?

9 7 9 8 9 9 9 2 3 3 6 8 4